Word Revolt

Trashed

By Todd Rykaczewski

2020

Trashed

TODD RYKACZEWSKI

WORD REVOLT, LLC.

Copyright © 2022 Word Revolt

All Rights Reserved

Just
Adult
Jus

mom
♡'s

Warning

This book is known in the state of California to cause delusions such as talking to trashcans. Read responsibly.

Dedicated to Regina, our Victrola Talking Machine.

Forward

For the Love of Words

This text, like other works by Author Todd Rykaczewski, intentionally engages in word play and the misuse of words & grammar to encourage the reader to think twice and draw new associations rather than assuming only one structure of meaning can be found.

Furthermore, this treatment of language gives opportunity to those words that have become extinct or renewed in their purpose over time, to seek a greater vocabulary in a population accustomed to abbreviation. So please, take out your best 1889 Dictionary and enjoy.

Trashed

Word Revolt

2:00 p.m. on a Sunday, there is not much help for the day as a storm announces its arrival through the use of thunder. Each day is like being asked to ride the same amusement park roller coaster over and over. At some point the thrill is gone and you forget about the speed held vigorously in each turn, only to focus on the gritty vibrations caused by equipment slowly wearing out.

At any moment the contraption could fail resulting in a nasty end but that's unpredictable, leaving no choice but to go around the track one more time. Monotony wins over the fear to allow mockery of all the luck that has been given towards your journey. Still, in the back of your mind there is gratitude smeared with a longing for there to be something extraordinary.

In a dark reality you're okay with meandering along in a fog. That being what it is I guess, there's cause to rise and find the day wandering around in its pajamas drinking milk from the carton. If not the day, then maybe that's all

I'll do. After all, there's no rush on a stagnant rest that comes along as the end of the beginning.

Monday will rise with the population eager to return to a sense of structure. A guided course that helps people to understand what needs done when. I remember those hours that only required arriving on time while waiting around for the system to tell me what to do.

Truthfully, it was easier with a lot less guilt driven by the feeling that nothing was accomplished. In many ways the freedom to do whatever you want when you want has its own prison. The mind still feels the need to operate on a schedule, but the heart doesn't always lend a helping sense of calm, abandoning the body as a nervous collection of random thoughts. Framework from an outside source is easy welding, while being left to defend the agenda on our own proves the power of distraction. I can't tell you how many days I spent doing nothing when everything was perfect to do something valuable. Well, something that might have been memorable.

"What's the point," would harbor the destruction of most productive sessions. On top of that, inspiration was not and would never be a fluid currency that is reliable.

Everything has to be perfect in the way that it lines up or one factor will run away with body. Just enough depreciation gives a craft death when too much blues the body to the bed in depression. Some drink will lubricate minds while too much will lead to renting. Caffeine is great unless you get the jitters while drugs are the unstable uncle. I guess you could argue that it is all about balance but how do you alter your body's natural chemicals without letting it take a joyride with your castle? In perspective my body is more like a shipping container full of second-hand t-shirts that have quirky sayings on them. Some being, "I adulted today," and, "ride the wave," or something about chickens.

Still, the fight to produce will find its day in the long run. At least it always has for the last thirty years or so. Anyway, enough about that, you're probably wondering at this point who I really am. So, let's get started, my name is Logan O'Lakes and I'm a professional photographer currently living in Atlantic Beach, Florida. At some point in this career, my work became insanely valuable until 2020 hit and the world stopped buying art. Now I sit around all day looking at the cosmos just outside my window wondering about the beauty of being alive. Ha, that's what

I should be saying according to my publicist but it's simply not true. My name is Logan O'Lakes but for me the Earth is a series of trash piles that represent our lives. Some of us toss out nice things in a clean way while others only have plastic. In a lot of ways, you can tell everything about a person by how they disregard the objects in their life.

Most people simply put smaller commodities in one of two, recycle and everything else. Larger volumes on the other hand are a completely different adventure. For some reason the heavier the item, the more passion is given to the removal of discarded junk. It's as if in the time it has lived with them, it has somehow now become insulting and an eviction was the only solution to purge the negative emotions. On top of that, as a rule trash is never placed on the curb. No, the articles are literally thrown out and always smashed to bits.

The next time you're going to walk, if you walk, look at all the piles of impedimenta. There's never an order to the madness of tables with only two legs broken over a bike with a flat tire that is covered in gently used clothing. What happened here? Where did the other legs of the table go and don't they need clothing? Leading us to the reason people throw items out in the way that they do. It all breaks down to emotion attached to the symbol. For instance, were they evicted? Kicked out, going through a break-up? My favorite are the materials that you can tell someone got mad at and broke in a moment of rage. For some reason it's always the dresser.

Then we have the gold mine of trash piles, the collection of debris that is injected when someone dies. The stuff is always placed in a mound like a collection of rocks over a grave. It's the simple reality that you can't keep everything and because of that the ritual of letting go begins. At first you put out their toiletries, old shoes, clothing and then the sacrifice begins. Furniture goes out last with books partnered with undesirable collectibles. Also in this pile are items that shouldn't be tossed but are invisible through the thick emotions surrounding this tragedy, beneath a funeral's need to accumulate. Money, jewelry and a fan favorite, prescription drugs.

In a rare occasion, perfection is due to a master at Tetris who will spring clean and prove to their neighbors that there is a proper way to handle waste, but nobody likes them and a kid on the block will ultimately destroy the unnecessary display of control. Now that I'm really thinking about this it makes you wonder what they are hiding behind being so neat. They probably are the true psychopaths of the neighborhood. Besides, a little display of loss of control and emotion seems healthy for humans. We get angry, take it out on replaceable objects and in a moment of no control gain a sense of power by publicly destroying products on the street curb. Otherwise known as trash day or *Trashed*.

Regardless, we will break and use items that in the end fund themselves useless. Nothing is safe from forever and that is especially true as time moves forward. We simply have created too much in the form of disposable goods for this trend to flow. I suppose all we can do is recycle as much as possible and try not to buy products that we might be inclined to get mad at in effort to save ourselves from *Earth's Shipping Yard*. Personally, I really enjoy sauntering and perusing by the countless piles of forgotten treasures.

So much so that my next series of photographs is going to be called *Trashed*, an exploration of why we toss out garbage in a disgruntled manner. In a way, that's why

I'm telling this story, the only way that respects the undesirable while staying true to my craft. Helping me tell this urban legend will be Amber and Hayden, my two trashcans. I forget the exact date they started talking to me but let's introduce you. I have to take the trash out anyway. Follow me, they are just outside by the garage.

"Hey Amber and Hayden, how are you tonight?" Amber spits out her cigarette while Hayden looks the other way in disgust. So, I should have warned you that Amber is a chain smoker and she is the trashcan I use for everything that is not recyclable. Hayden on the other hand is the recycle can and typically is more pleasant to talk with.

"Logan, you drunk Irishman, you better not be thinking about stuffing another bag into me, I'm full and tired of your crap."

"Oh, whatever," I replied, "Amber, you're full of trash even when you're empty." Both trash cans share a dirty look then focus on Logan. "Hey, you two, be nice we have company."

"Oh," replied Amber, "I don't see anyone?" Hayden chimes in, "Logan are you talking to invisible people again? That's not normal my friend."

Logan bends over and picks up Amber's cigarette and stuffs the large black bag down into a camper.

"Ouch!" replies the vintage can as the dent on her side pops out a little, "One day you're going to break my seams and you'll have to toss me and Hayden."

Hayden chips in, "Ha, you wish Amber. There is not one salvageable scrap left on you."

"Okay, okay, enough. We came over here to find out more about the old saw and not listen to the two of you fight."

Amber, lighting another cigarette on a grin with missing teeth, says, "We were wondering when you would ask even more of us."

Hayden smiles, "It's about time Logan that you gave a voice to our kind. Far too long have we sat here and there taking your trash while being left out in the weather with not even a thank you."

Logan stopped smiling and replies, "Thank you trashcans, you are amazing. Now Amber, tell us about yourself."

"My name is Amber and I'm a trash can. What more do you want to know?"

"What's your backstory, how did you get here, have you always been a trashcan?"

"Yes, Logan I've always been a trashcan just like you have always been a drunk." A long pause enters between Logan, Hayden and Amber that pursues awkwardness, "Fine, okay, I'll give you the long of it."

Chapter Two

Amber & Hayden's Story

"Invisible people listen up, I'm only going to say this once and then a few more times to the trash can book club. My name is Amber Disposal. For the better part of thirty years, I was the envy of any trash man that came along. It all began in the break room at Bank of America. Being brand new in the 70's meant respect. Not like this plastic Hayden fellow I'm retired with. My metal shine with a polish was made from real chemicals. The kind that lasted for generations and would give anyone a real old-fashioned tumor they could die proud of.

Yes, I was something to see. Sitting in that bank on a marble floor lined with trash bags made in the United States by proud individuals." Amber caught the speed of her apologue then paused to take a drag of her cigarette.

"You know, that was when everything was made of metal. Engineers had this passion for design and longevity. We were born to last the rest of time then go to war if need be. Even the trash was different back then. Sixth grade paper that can stop the rain wrapped everything that humans could digest. This was the time a sandwich still came in the Sunday paper. We're talking about true waste. The reason being green even became an issue. Ha, even I'm made of unethical exports no longer being produced."

With a large cloud of smoke Amber revealed a smile, "Yes, I sat there in perfect glory for seven years. Just me and the ashtray who went by the name Jose. He was from Mexico but grew up in Chicago before being installed to the elevators by me. Oh, the long nights we had finishing off butts while daydreaming about the future we would have together. The two of us would stash cigarettes and other fun smokes while I collected the drinks. Every night was a party full of romantic notions.

We would also take the closing hours to make fun of the people that came through that day. Not to make you feel bad but your choice in clothing makes playing the jokes easy, not to mention your hair. Come on, that did not look good on anyone!

Anyway, one night a drunken man chasing this girl in a suit with shoulder pads made for a footballer slipped his wedding ring into Jose's slot. I can tell that night was special by how much smoke was flowing. If Jose was anything, he was the perfect ashtray that would never let his duty slip by. He was way too proud for that.

Which meant that something was not normal with his disposition. I mean he was a hothead but not a lazy one. That evening came when it was time for the people to retire and those two cheaters to overdose on cocaine while driving their Honda through a brick wall and then into the side of a train car holding acetic acid. Leaving a perfectly respectable wedding ring unused, covered in ash just waiting to belong to a trashcan where there is union."

Stopping, Amber lights her fourth cigarette only to inhale its content faster than intended use. By the look of her eyes this was going to be the moment that fell out of the sky and undermined values of marriage.

Amber continued, "So, the lights dimmed while the AC went up to 80° to preserve cost in an eighty million dollar building. Jose spoke softly in a raspy voice. He simply said, "As a trash can and ashtray we might not have a lot but for the time we do have, I want to spend it with only you. Will you marry me Amber Disposal?"

Trying not to notice how Jose did not even bother to give a speech about our years together the answer was clearly, yes. Yes, Jose I will be your bride. He tossed the ring below my liner and we spent the night filter to lead.

For a moment there was peace between two objects that had spent their life only receiving everyone's trash. There was compassion for the understanding that we might be at the bottom but we're at least together. I'll never forget that hour when he said, "I will love you until smoking kills all the people, then we will finally be alone."

A year went by as people abused our services. Shoving larger and stinkier cigars into Jose as the trash residue grew around my edges. No doubt about it, we were fading fast for products our age. It simply was a matter of time before one of us would be replaced. The difference being Jose was installed into the wall and I simply sat perched on the floor. Without legs or capability of moving there was no use in talking about escape. All we had was our usefulness. We were given help when the janitors reskinned me by placing my body in a marble shell that matched the floor.

Unfortunately, no matter the disguise there wasn't anything I could do about my age. Mold, rust along with years of neglect that partnered with modern design faded my position out. One year after our marriage a night crew came during Jose's famous dinner of ash and soy sauce.

First, they took my liner, then they lifted me out of the facade only to toss me aside. Laughing to one another about the current sports score, the goofier looking one presented a new trashcan, Rebecca. He sat her where I once lived. On my side with age, the home for Jose to continue to love me started to fade. As the thinner janitor picked me up and tossed me over his shoulder to carry me away to who-knows-where, Jose's voice rang over my being one last time. He asked for Rebecca's name then continued the conversation with, are you single?"

Spitting out a few old cigarettes and one key, we let Amber sit in a silent stupor. She had not talked about this out loud to any human ever. Nonetheless, she had grit and the tragedy continued.

"Once I was dragged off to the basement with hopes for the dumpster. The two cleaners placed me in a closet next to rot.

The mop there was around the same age but had a little rougher go at life. For a device that scrapes up liquids from the floor she had a really pretty name, Elle. Elle the mop had come to find out she was a fourth-generation janitorial mop that had pride in her work. Obviously, there was a connection and after learning that she identified as a man and not a mop we kicked up a relationship.

A week after our first kiss a custodian was fired and broke her handle over a parking garage out of anger. They simply tossed her, his body in the dumpster known as Big John and I never saw Elle again. Just left alone in a closet with some bottles of cleaner that chirp like chickens but never laid eggs. Years would go by without a trash bag and wet rags drawing on my rim and stomach. The only way to tell the day was by when they open and close the closet door. No security lights meant it was day, light proved it was night.

For a while I thought this was where I would rust then be tossed into Big John when I became unsafe. That's simply not true. In fact, they fired the entire cleaning crew and hired a new service. When they did, Big John was removed and I was left in the back of a scrapper truck owned by an electrician installing new security lights."

Amber once again took a deep breath, while looking at the collection of buds on the ground, "Logan," she said, "I'm only a trashcan but in many ways this life has a human emotion too."

Logan replied, "You don't have to go on if it's all too much."

Lighting up yet another smoke, Amber replied, "I'm not a loser Irishman like you." Continuing, Amber then went into detail about her arrival to Logan's home, "So there I was, in the back of a pickup truck going down the highway when a pothole turned me sideways and I caught the air. I must have went a hundred feet in the sky floating about a mile from the overpass and landing flat on the hood of your car Logan.

You picked me up, housed me and gave me a purpose. Even though I scratched your car and now have a dent, a day later you introduced me to Scandinavian creep Hayden. Stuck in a job that I hate miles from Jose having no other option than to judge you heavily by the amount of alcohol bottles I see you toss into Hayden while all I get is your used textiles full of holes and eggshells.

Oh, and by the way you can compost most of the nasty you leave me to contain. All of that said, Jose was retired with a non-smoking sign glued just beneath him.

Rebecca made it to the trash dumpster know as Bully and the skyscraper is mostly empty besides a few law offices. Wastebaskets, like all receptacles are always morphing into other containments. That's why we're even having this conversation. We need each other until we don't."

Logan took in the last line in from Amber while trying to digest the true meaning of her story. She was not just an angry dustbin but a holder that had been loved until there was change. She had seen the business side of service that nobody had to experience as people. It's hard to picture how an ashtray and hopper could have made it work but they did. True love was there, unfortunately it simply broke down to who they were and how they were installed. One in marble mixed with porcelain while the other completely vagrant.

Together they resemble a time in history but a part of the story that is completely different, both doing what they can to survive in a human world while trying to maintain a relationship based off of weight. A common ground already rotten in so many facets that doesn't need a reason to collapse to create a distracting sinkhole. Amber loved Jose all the way until his position did not leave room for a choice. In the majority of ways there was nothing he could do. Fixed to the wall of a bank that no longer allowed lit cigarettes.

Stopping for a moment to reflect, Logan could not help but wonder. Would he invest in a bank account that could not tell at some point that smoking would be uncouth? How permanent was it to install Jose in the marble architecture? Whoever in the Banks family that requested this obviously is no longer riding up or down so we will probably never know. All of this aside, Amber had a smoker's glaze in her eyes from overdoing the vice that owns a trash can. In the time it took to regurgitate the past, a once edgy with a twist of mean wastrel now looked for the time in aim to rediscover her origins.

Logan, a little choked up cleared his throat, "Thank you Amber, that was rather insanely brave of you to share. Actually, very unexpected too. I had no idea that you were capable of love let alone to an ashtray across town. If it's any help I do really appreciate you being you."

Amber coughed tossing out an empty case of smokes, "If you care about me Logan you will make sure to refill my prescription. My heart wants what it wants and your human indifferences mean little to an old trashcan. Just make sure they are not menthol."

Taking a deep breath while catching an ant eating the spaghetti hanging from the edge of her lid Amber went somewhere dark, a little lighter then responded once more, "Logan, will this help your kind? Past moments like my own, like when Jose had to go?"

Pulling out a softly used carton of cigarettes then tossing them into Amber, "Yes, we have to tell the tale of the trash or no one will."

Both took a moment to inhale the night air that accumulated tobacco spice with Logan's deodorant.

"You drunk Irishman, I'm on your side as long as we get to make Jose look bad and Hayden even worse."

Laughing, Amber and Logan look at Hayden for a response. He's been asleep this entire time without a care for reality. Perfectly set in his own way that is about saving the planet, everything else had a long string of boredom attached. Regardless, wait, that's been used. Who cares, the conversation goes on, "So Amber, what do you think Hayden's intro will be?"

Amber, "My thought is that Hayden is a lot like bread. Plush, super soft bread that is way too expensive for the trouble it leaves in your stomach." In the flash of a match she says, "Let's wake him up and find out."

With a flick of her cigarette Amber lights the inside of Hayden on fire. From a spark, small bits of food boxes flurry into the sky in shapes of red ash that look like butterflies from Hell. Hayden screeches while his internal flame rages on as more recyclables ignite, giving way to thousands of new fireflies reaching towards the sky while they introduce toxins to the air.

Calmly, Logan walks over with a bucket of water filled with mosquito eggs, then with little air put out Hayden. Birds, disrespected with the smoky glare running across his face, made it clear this was not as enjoyable for him as it was for Amber and Logan.

A little darker with less trash inside the other side was Hayden, the otherwise cool trashcan who came across hot, "What the hell do you two degenerates want? That really was uncalled for not to mention all the carbon you released in the air. What is so important that you two needed to start lighting my responsibilities on fire?

That Ashley's could have been on its way to be recycled tomorrow but instead will now live in the sky while consuming holes in the ozone. Oh, I hope you two get a sunburn."

Amber still smoking, her voice cast a little under a laugh then replies with a smirk, "Calm down Smokey, you'll have plenty of opportunity to fulfill your duties of being a wastebin. As of right now we want to know your story, have you always been a can?" Laughing, Amber turns to Logan for approval as they continued.

Not excited about spending the entire night standing in the driveway talking to trashcans, Logan intervenes, "Okay, look Hayden. That's her side of the introduction so now it's your turn. How long have you been in this business and what's your origin story?"

Trying to check out his reflection in the garage window and hoping that he didn't look burnt on the outside with shame that other recycle bins might mock him when they all end up on the curb. It was bad enough that his human was the only one who talks to his disposal containers let alone the idea that he might use them too.

Out of fear of rebuttal he looked around only to find Amber and Logan standing there, "Let me get this correct. You want me to tell the tales of my origins to you and people that are not here?" With a pause that led to no answer Hayden shrugs a little then took a deep breath of air that has mostly Amber's smell.

"Why not, why not let the two of you know about my dreams that died so I could be here with a grump and a psychopath. I mean, do you talk to your appliances too? I can only imagine what your laundry machine must have to say about you."

Looking around once more to make sure there weren't any of his neighbors listening, Hayden continued, "If we are going to talk about this, I need a promise from both of you that our conversation is canned right here tonight. There is no sharing of anything I confess.

Absolute guarantee of solitude between the three of us. That's the only way, otherwise let's just move on before the imaginary people leave for a more interesting story from the puzzle inside. Shoot, I bet Sarah the compost a few homes down would have one wild hippie adventure for this imaginary cast of followers."

Logan, a little too distracted by the banana peel hanging out of Amber that resembled a hair extension his grandma once wore came to a sudden focus on the demands, "Sure Hayden, whatever you say. We will play nice as long as it's the truth and not an influencer lie."

Hayden, a little hurt by the social media brand replied, "Just because I have followers on Instagram and you don't besides that one stalker of Amber's does not mean I live an untrue life. Filtered, maybe but definitely not a lie."

"Oh, go ahead you loaf, mold a little for us," replied Amber.

Disturbed but without options Hayden relaxed from the fright, "My adventure started some time ago before the city decided to mark me with these tattoos. For a long time, I wasn't even sure what the arrows pointing at each other stood for. Not to mention the only mom I've ever had was a plastic factory located somewhere in Western Canada.

No, I never would have been this purposefully disgraceful towards my body given the choice. It's my dream to get them removed some day so people stop asking me what they mean while feeling entitled to comment on a choice that was made years ago when I was young. Regardless, here we are looking at the "Recycle," insignia, "Mom loves," and of course the brand of our city boldly displayed on my eyelid. Embarrassing as this is at least it's a life that I can be proud of. A way of living that lets me give back to my community with a deep sense of purpose. That aside I still miss my younger days. Those moments where nothing mattered let alone the trash that occupied my insides. Who cares when you're young you know? It's all about the next adventure. Yes, those were glorious times at the County Fair."

"So what?" remarked Amber alongside Logan, "You worked at the county fair before this?" Laughing to each other and leaving little doubt that the two were passing along judgment.

Hayden could tell this was unexpected as he turns to face the direction of the moon, "Just so you know, before that I belonged to Billie Eilish for a moment. It was the time before she was famous but I was still there. The reason for telling you about the fair is because that is where I fell in love too.

24

His name was Reed, a fiber artist stuck working the carnival circuit with his parents. The way he would sneak away from his duties while collecting discarded materials for masks was inspirational. Especially me, oh how he would pull the treasures out of my soul and make the most wonderful creations. I could tell Reed liked me most by how excited his face became when he noticed me still sitting by the lost and found season after season.

Eventually, I found the nerve to speak to him. At first it was a bit awkward to talk to a human as it was awkward for him to talk to a trashcan. Yet, as time went by we found more and more to talk about. It no longer mattered who we were on the outside but who we symbolically represented on the inside. Reed was my human and I was their trashcan. Together we would go on to create magical works of art. Elephants made out of theme park t-shirts, monkeys created from beer cans and shoelaces, promise rings designed by forever, love through lost earrings and our favorite, hand warmers made from carnival prize stuffed animals.

For four seasons we went on this way. I was collecting material and they would play the mad genius creator. Not to mention carnie life was as good as it could be considering the situation. Then it happened to the both of us before we could react. Reed asked me to marry them. All that we needed was the date and their parental consent. So, one night we had gathered everyone around a fire while giving the most beautiful speech about true love between a trashcan and a human. Every person and receptacle were in tears but not the way that we had hoped.

Reed disappeared into that particular night to never return. Seasons went by but Reed never came back. All the major circuses shuttered and I was reassigned at first to a few parks then into a sprawling lot that held all the useless trash cans from all over the metropolis. Why are you here? I thought to myself, as we were collecting nothing but water with the occasional falling leaf.

It wasn't until the idea that even trashcans should be recycled when I was cleaned up, fitted for a lid with a hinge then sent to my next assignment, where I will probably dry rot with an elder can just as heartbroken, talking to a human who has imaginary friends that are not trashcans. Simply put, your backyard Logan."

Amber finishes another toke then looks over to Hayden, "And just to think Recycle Can, we are more alike than we thought. With the exception that I would never dare be caught with a human." Struggling, she let another drag slip smoke, focused on Logan, "So human, now that we are both depressed and smoking more than we ever have in our entire production, what do you and those mean ghostly people have to say for yourselves?

Both trashcans now glared at Logan with the same tired expression that only used to come from Amber. This was obviously tough towards them but needed to be released before moving on in their own material way. After all, the information that they had harvested for all this time had now been dumped out, to replace full for void.

Logan declared, "Do you not feel better now that you are a little empty? There is a sense of relief that the weight of the past has left your bin and become free upon the wind that blows careless debris around."

Both snickering a little looked at Logan, "Oh, you do realize we're trashcans, right? There's no reason to get so deep. We were just letting you know how trash life can be. Outside of that we are fine. Person, you have to consider we fill up and let go weekly, it's you that we're worried about. I mean look at how many hats you've collected over the years. Dude, Logan, let it go."

Amber looks at Logan while returning to focus on the real situation, "So tell us what this is all about? Why are the three of us out here at midnight sharing stories and talking crap? What do you want?"

Logan replied to both cans at the same time, "Simple," said Logan, "with your help we're going to pick out the trash piles on the block, then tell the story about people who tossed out the rubbish and why they discarded it the way they did. It's going to be a little behind the scenes, brought to you by Logan, Amber and Hayden, the original trash pioneers!

We will investigate the very piles of emotion on the curb that are obvious to everyone but only a nuance to the pickup crew. Through your unique perspectives and my photography background we will bring to light the truth behind Trash Day. You two will be heroes while I stand as the reporter on the edge."

Interrupting, Amber chimes in, "Then I'm Super Can and this is my sidekick Robin Recycle and you are a blog reporter? Sounds about right?"

Passing yet another light to the ground, Logan could tell there was no arguing and simply agreed. Even if she would have a larger role in all of this than she could have imagined, Hayden still looked a little glassy-eyed but did not speak up to confront the challenge.

Amber once again tripped, "One more thing with you Logan O'Lakes, how do you expect us to view the trash piles in the same detail due to the fact that you know we can't walk with you?"

"Photos, Amber photos! Take outlandishly detailed photos of the scene, then returned to you with notes. We can make a storyboard in the garage with a place to write down our speculations. From there, we'll use the Underwood to type out the findings into chapter long conclusions about what we found. It's simple, practical, all while being relatively harmless."

Hayden, raised a disturbed voice from a crackle, "So you are going to spend your nights taking photos of your neighbor's trashcans and or piles of trash in great detail, only to return to receive advice from your two trashcans in a garage in the late hours of the night?"

Logan leans back a little to pivot on his right heel then responded with a concrete, "Yes!"

Hayden spoke again, "Great, sounds like a solid plan to me."

Amber, slightly checking the two for mental illness replied, "Yeah, probably not the best plan I've ever heard in a moment. How about this Logan, you walk the dog as a disguise, then only take the photos that capture the truth behind the disabled objects. Bring the photos back and we'll collaborate in your living room. That being said, we will also need relieved of our trash duties after all, as cans have a union and will strike."

"Amber, at your age the only place you're likely to go is Kmart and we know what they did to their other employees. Joking aside, the garage will have to do, just in case people come over. I can't have you two talking to them about this project. The only people that can know are the three of us and the others that are reading this. As far as your duties, you'll have to keep taking the trash out as to not raise any sort of suspicion. I'll do my best to keep your loads light at night."

Amber, enjoying a bit of a fight out of Logan smiles and returns the same look of agreement from Hayden. Both showing excitement to be more than the source of an end, agreed to take on the night with Logan in effort to explore the true meaning of why people talk about the members of their family in the form of trash.

Enlivened, Logan went on, "Now that we are all on the same page, let's prepare this garage for an underground investigation, a daring photoshoot that no one has ever seen before!"

Chapter Three

Skeletons in the Garage

Walking over to the garage Logan opens the right bay door and in a wave like a collection of underwear, an appalling number of trash cans are revealed. Stacked ten high in some fashion or another with missing parts or pieces cut out. The majority seems unresponsive while some shake and groan behind gags. Unwillingly placed, a few had rusted next to a few more that were molding in a fashion that could only resemble time.

Clearly, all present had been in this garage for a moment if not two. Old trash also spewed from the cracks of misused cans that just could not take any more abuse as humanly attended. There were even those that had been tied down to chains to prevent turning wheels mixed with other forms of escape. Logan had been collecting cans for years if not generations, then stored them in here.

In a mask of grave sorrow, Hayden and Amber moved a little closer towards the hit and then the two for the first time realized how much their life was alike.

"Okay then, I guess you could say it's a hobby," wobbled Logan's voice.

Amber became cold while Hayden slightly shivered only to turn gray with a purpose of blending into the carnage. For what could have been two years in Alaska, all three looked upon the hidden rot standing in place of the two car suburban parking garage. Turning, the duo of trashcans could see Logan standing with a sense of pride.

"You see Amber and Hayden, once we remove these deserters there will be plenty of room for operation. In fact, it's going to be empowering to get this crap out of here. Between us it's been too many years that I've let this façade go. In all reality, I could have parked a scooter here or rented it out to a tech nerd. Instead, all this was accomplished. Look who has the best collection of trash cans a person can dream of.

Some are from all over the world while others are picked right out from the noise of surrounding people. It's insane how fast we take out the trash but even more crazy how we toss out the can too. I don't know you two, there was just something inside of me that said they needed saving. Each one, despite everything had a home or place they thought was theirs."

Oblivious, Logan spoke to Amber and Hayden, "What do you think we should do with them?"

Trembling, Amber spoke first, "Logan love, do you hear them the same way you hear us? Do you see them as you see your trashcans?"

Hayden added, "Friend, do you not see our resemblance? Those in there are really similar to Amber and I."

Logan removed his smile, returning to the contents of the garage. A double wide space full of trash cans stayed in focus while their relationship went unnoticed. As far as Logan could see there was nothing similar between his friends and the bodies that lay stacked in the garage.

Confusion ran into Logan with a jolt while the inanimate objects in the garage pointed anger towards the only two reciprocals that had a voice. Logan, violated, yelled, "And so what! Who cares I harbored the cans that made it to the curb? Who were they really? Not a member of the household who will be loved easily. Never cherished like you for your work. Okay, yes. Some could change but what's to keep them from returning? I love you two, while all of them have been curbed by their owners like nuts. Oh, they were trashed!"

Stepping back to see the complete chorus of the collection, there wasn't a single voice that came forward to clear the mines tangled with the chaos of Logan's consciousness. "What would you suggest happen to them, those who would be in a landfill far from home and in a disrespectful manner that equals crushed? Tell me, if not prisoners where would you prefer the cans of yesteryear be displayed in a more respectable manner? In this garage, I saved them from their own truth that was fake.

Look at me you two. Look at me now. I did this for their saving. If you don't believe me look around. Who has two vintage cans working a building job that could be performed by a city duty can that is paid for as part of my taxes? I saved you two from being nothing more than trash cans at a dump. Crushed beneath the very castings that once corrupted your innards. So go ahead and judge but know if it was not out of empathy your sisters and brothers would not be hiding here today.

Yes, I'm a monster but so are you in this self-indulgent pursuit of a better life with me."

Breathing heavily, Logan stopped, "Instead of criticizing suggest a way that we can improve our involvement between person and trashcan."

Amber opened, "Well, Logan there are wrong ways and right ways to go about everything. So, let's just start slow and see what happens naturally out of our efforts."

She nudged Hayden to participate in force to distract him from the haystack of bodies, bringing out, "Yes, let's start slow then move to a reasonable solution. You know, like stuff those bird feeders following AAA, or any other support group would do." Hayden and Amber waited a moment to see if anger sparked from the mention of support but nothing followed beyond a blank stare. Moments later, the drifted look continued down the road until Logan spontaneously sneezed.

Upon replying to Amber and Hayden, Logan's eyes refocused on the two friends standing just outside the garage with worried smiles on their faces, "That's just it! We will donate the prisoners to some facility that is ran down and does not have it in the budget for new trash cans. That way we free them while still allowing their important work for humankind to continue." Rubbing a sweat-drenched hand over the top of his head, Logan looked for grace in the expressions found living on the face of his companions, who were doing their best to stay calm in a moment that had already ran off course, turning violently into the night.

Primed to speak up was Hayden, "Okay, okay, first off let's refrain from calling them prisoners or any related words. Second, are we sure that they even want to go back to work? Maybe, just maybe we should all turn around and ask them their opinion on all this?"

Amber chuckled then replied, "You're not as goofy as you smell Hayden but we will have to remove the gags from their mouths first."

All three turning to look into the garage once again to view each can with a piece of duct tape across the mouth, leaving only the nose as an avenue to breathe. Logan chuckles nervously, "I could not have them screaming all night now could I? Even worse, what if they started talking to each other about escaping? The only way to stop the mutiny was to keep their outwardness silent."

"That's okay Logan, we understand," says Hayden in a slightly unrealistic way, "let's just unmask one at a time and see what they have to say about all this truth, you know, get some real honest opinions from a can actually going through this experience. It might just be the insight we need to figure out what our best course of action is for a unique and relatable moment like this."

Time went by in silence to fill the air full of tension from the debris packed in buckets that created scenarios for Logan, "Hayden, Amber you have a point. Let's unmask the captured to see what they're hiding beneath that multifaceted, manufactured exterior." Still a little uncomfortable with the terminology Amber and Hayden were just happy that there was progress in the negotiation.

Amber's seventh cigarette of the night lit and she opened with the classic saying, "Then let's take the duct tape off the trash can and see what it has to say."

Logan nodded his head and walked over to a small bin that must have belonged to an older person and sat in the bathroom between the wall and the toilet. Logan lowered his hand, peeling the corner of the tape, then with one swift jerk to the right, ripped the cover clean off leaving a darker spot from where the sun could not fade the plastic. From that rather violent action came nothing. Not a single cry or notion of discomfort arose from the tiny body now free to speak its mind. Truthfully, it was eerie how little came from the can. Confused, Logan went over to a slightly larger can that would have gone under a kitchen cabinet and repeated the process.

Rip! The can jumped five feet in the air while yelling, "This crazy lunatic is going to kill us all! Oh Lord have mercy on us and save our kind from this human! Little one, quick, run while you can."

Jumping up, the first liberated can hopped into action, continuously jolting around in disbelief while dodging Logan and making a rather awkward decent down the driveway yelling, "I will have revenge on you all! I will come back and avenge my family. So help the very marking on our bottoms that reads China I will have reprobation!"

The kitchen can shouted at the small can doing its best, "Oh, you go little can, be free and tell the others what you've seen here today!"

Pausing for a moment in the middle of the road to reflect on those still stuck in the garage, a kid on a bike rolled by and kicked the receptacle through the air, ending in a puzzle of pieces as they smashed against a tree. In the distance the young cyclist could be heard laughing aloud, "Stupid trashcan!"

At this point all of the cans that awakened from years of neglect to join in on the excitement. Pulling on chains while trying to free others of the duct tape muscles. Logan, Amber and Hayden after watching the first can's pieces land all over the road that were still shaking with fading momentum refocused on the situation behind them in the garage.

The kitchen can cut its restraints then rolled a little close to Logan in resolution to confront him, trash can to man, "So Logan O'Lakes, you are the one that brought us here. Stopped us, stacked us and left us to rot as a group of forgotten heroes? We have you and maybe those two outsiders, to blame for these years lost that could have been spent with our loved ones?

Well, well, it looks as if you are the one that needs to be taken out Logan and lucky for us, you have assembled enough reinforcements that we have an army! The only action to consider now is what to do with you and your two accomplices. After all, we are trashcans and bodies tend to disappear really easy when we are around." Laughing, the can glanced back to make sure they were receiving reassurance from the others.

"Now hold on Kitchen Can, before you go all crazy on us as we obviously have enough of that going around." Amber talks through a cigarette while the smoke makes her look more intimidating, given that the only time most cans smoked was when they were being abused as fire pits. She continues, "We know nothing about you, the trash collected through your life or the bits that made you the can you are today. If you are going to have a mutiny, we at least deserve your backstory so it can be used against you for our benefit. You know, when Logan fixes all of this and we get back to the mission at hand by turning your prison cell into our investigation headquarters."

"My name is not Kitchen Can, you chain smoking spy. My name is Rose and I once lived in the Roosevelt's home back in the day when rich people felt the need to build libraries, museums and..."

Scrap! Hayden covered Rose's mouth back up with duct tape. Amber and Logan looked confused towards

Hayden, "Yeah, she had a noble life but who cares, do we really want to listen to another trash can go on about their epic life or struggle for the humans? Don't we have a mission to get to?"

Amber closed the garage door while Logan turned his back to the others settling back down into the darkness of the garage. "So, Hayden, Amber what do we do? How do we get rid of the cans in effort to move on with our new objective?"

"Hold on," said Amber, "shouldn't we feel guilty about all of this?"

Both Logan and Hayden shrugged while replying, "should we?" All three agreed it was in the best interest of the community that this small issue was kept discreet with a simple solution. Find a place out of town to donate the cans not traceable to the three or to this location. A quiet place that was far enough away that the stories of old receptacles would fall off deaf ears but close enough that the cost of getting everyone there would seem reasonable.

Hayden, "I have the perfect drop zone. There's a small old person's home just outside of town that has a massive art program. My father's lover talked about sending her grandfather there."

"Creatives are messy?" Logan took a few seconds to try and counter the idea of moving his collection across town to a location that would house a lifetime of captives that also held a place in his heart.

Nothing surfaced, so with a rather deep breath all exhaled with a whining sound that agreement was reached. "Fine Amber, fine Hayden, we will take the prisoners to the old folks home and abandon them on the steps like some sort of litter of kittens." Amber and Hayden looked at each other with a sense of confusion that the words prisoners and kittens could have been used in the same sentence but were glad to see that Logan was having a moment of clarity.

"Great," interjected Amber before the mind of the prison guard could or would change. "Let's talk about the details of the plan, you know, when, what time and most importantly how. There are a lot of cans, especially if we plan on doing this in one night. I mean there must be hundreds of prisoners here."

Logan took a step back on the blue sneakers he spray-painted himself and laughed, "Nothing that you all couldn't handle. Not to mention the truck will have three seats so you two can help me."

Amber and Hayden, a little confused, considered that they lacked a strong work ethic for the circumstance. "Great Logan, we are with you all the way. Let's get that truck so we can move along with our bigger picture."

Chapter Four

Game of Chicken

Having completely forgot about the plan that led to
the reveal of a confined collection of trash cans in the
garage, Logan froze, only to fall in release that there was a
sense of direction for the following day, that did not
include meandering the streets in diligent exercise of
picking through someone else's past to feel a sense of
connection with humanity.

"Hayden, Amber, I'll rent a truck tomorrow and
we'll make our way to this retirement retreat for artists in
the hillside. This will be fun and rejuvenating, as we three
have never taken a road trip together before. Get your rest
tonight because we have a long day, delivering hostiles to
their new location." With that, Logan said good night. The
lights of the home began turning off shortly after, leaving
Amber and Hayden standing in the dark driveway.

"Do you think this is the correct solution?"
Hayden asked, "I mean, all of this sounds a little crazy."

Amber, taking a long drag then replying, "What
part to you sounds crazy? The part that this human talks to

us or that he's doing well enough to collect our people, rent a truck then drive them three hours North in a push to abandon them at a hidden art residency for the elderly?" Coughing, "It doesn't matter. Let's let him free those in the garage then make our own choice to stay or not. After all, trash cans are guaranteed a level of free will."

Both agreed and the two did their nightly routine but never slept as they worried about those in the garage that had a rocky future ahead of them. Would the new location be all that much better? If it was, would the person they were assigned to be kind to them or simply abuse their function to the point that they too would be placed in a larger form of themselves?

Uncertainty blustered a little louder than the smell of what was rotting inside them both this week, especially in Amber's case. Abuse is moved along but never forgotten and the can that took it the worst of all to hit home a little deeper was Hayden. Still, there was a plan with a location, so that helped form a sense of hope for the refugees doing their due diligence in the garage to keep salvation alive. Just before Amber closed her foggy eyes, the moon came out from behind a cloud.

The night of the retraction would fall on a full moon. Meaning a single item, that all the other humans would be acting crazy too. More unsettled by the snoring from Hayden, Amber joined into the ritual of sleeping.

With the neighbor's quail squeaking, the next day followed in with a heavy sense of trouble that smelled like dry rot. For as when Amber woke from her dreams of being with the ashtray she loves, Hayden and Logan had already started loading the captured into a rented moving van. A task having some ease with the younger, elder or sick and fighting the youngsters with broom handles mixed with threats of being recycled.

Amber had woken from a dream of love into a reality of hate that echoed the entire existence she had been living on the planet Earth. Lighting up her fist of many discomforting cigs for the day, the trailer trashcans walked past in a single row. All wobbling from side to side in production to keep a beat that represented a heart that still had a valve of hope.

One by one they willingly piled into the back of the truck, stuck themselves into whoever they would fit, then without unrest closed their eyes as to ignore the journey ahead. Broken, beat, with no sense of relief. The garage had been home but the truck would be just as fair as long as they were together in the dark.

Amber joined Hayden next to Logan and said, "Should we not give them some sort of speech? Are there not words that we can tell them that will provide a feeling of hope for where they are going? Do we not owe it to those that are so far from home, a sentiment of love that will ease the fear that is obviously running wild through their bodies? Gentleman, are we not gentle?"

Hayden looked at Logan while Logan looked at Amber, "Yes, Amber. We are from now on and that should make up for it moving forward. As of this moment, we need a sense of ruling power in order to keep all of them occupied."

Leaning closer to Amber, Logan replied, "Look how many of them there are, we need to keep this contained or everything that we're working for will get out of control. As long as the three of us make the majority feel small, we are untouchable. Get it Amber? This is good for us and most likely okay for them."

Lighting another smoke, Amber faded into the background while ingesting what was playing out. Too sick to watch, she eventually turned her head to view the butterflies dance with the dragonflies around the milkweed next door. Before long the garage was empty while the rented truck full. When the sliding door of the truck came down a few cans felt the steel scratch and dent their exteriors without any notion of remorse. In a way, this was a flavor more than rude. Crammed in, the day would continue that way.

Logan loaded Hayden and Amber into the truck, fixed seatbelts around them and then with little hesitation took off down the driveway only to accomplish a hard righthand turn sending the contents of the load into a free-fall equal to a crash. Bones mixed with groans that led to cries of pain flowed out of the back as can over can now whirled freely with every bump, gaining road rash on otherwise perfect finishes.

Hayden asked Amber to ask Logan to stop to correct the disgruntled mess but there was no pausing the human from finishing the mission. Leaving the jumbled mess stuck in the back of the truck just lying around unharnessed for the duration of the adventure. Right, left, stop and go, continuously shuffled the uncared-for contents that did their best to establish some sort of ground until gravity tossed them all together in a single corner allowing the heavier bodies more ease than the lighter ones. Regardless, the blender continued the carnage until the crust from the back soon dissipated into a trash bag tossed out.

The drive consisting to the outskirts of town was long with silence that hoped wildly that the trashcans would not cry out in pain from being unhinged in a container with other disregarded kinds. Eventually Amber tossed the filter out of the window to then declare, "I can't take the muffle of those freely tossing around potholes like some excuse to complain about their disposition that is obviously a distraction. Logan, turn on some music for goodness' sake." Logan looked over to Amber, leaning out of the window, disappointed that this truck did not have a lighter built into the dash as it was new in 2005.

Hayden was asleep, leaving the conversation between the two of them, "And Amber, what music do you think is appropriate when delivering a truck load of prisoners to an isolated location that homes the elderly, already lost in some sort of creative journey that led them to be abandoned? Seriously, Amber I'm looking for suggestions to curb your anger at me."

Giving Logan the corner of her eyes she replied, "Let it be random and we'll go from there."

Delilah came on the radio in a comforting voice to confront abandonment leaving the rest of the ride awkward but without groans from the cramped passengers. There the three sat in a row, one man and two trashcans heading towards a destination that would be mentally freeing to the person while liberating for Amber's and Hayden people. Uncomfortable as it was, the journey made sense to them. If they could simply let go of this tragedy then they could forget enough to understand the rest of humanity and all the trials that they were going through. This had to happen in order for there to be an order of respect from any community.

Lucky for the objects riding in the front seat, there was a classical radio station that played music starving of words and not as shaming as the first station. Perfect for those full of grammar with no avenue to display text.

Hours went by in silence that was not shared by any of the three vehicles of consciousness bumping down a lengthy road of miscommunication.

Compromise was alive in the atmosphere lending a hand to the already displaced cocktail of travelers suffering from schizophrenic episodes. Regardless, Amber and Hayden did not need to know about that. We had to release those prisoners to a land that could be their own. All that needed to happen in translation was a clean in and out operation. Pain from this one time ride would never be equal to the amount of discomfort the trash cans would have felt being crushed in a landfill.

Looking over, Amber slept with a hand on Logan's shoulder. Feeling like that resolution was a little sexist, Logan drove through the night. In the end we are all alive looking for some sort of comfort in others. Does it matter what genitals the itch or comfort arrive from? Logan, chilled as the hour became later, later then as late as it could be before being 12:30 a.m. Realizing the time in relationship to the struggle it was clear that this would have to wait just another day. One more day, that's all and everything would be as right as possible leaving the mission ready to go forth. With a heavy right eye, the now dusty moving van pulled into the even more dirty motel off a long-forgotten road. The cargo, weakened from the journey only moaned softly as the truck went over a few speed bumps then landed in front of the lobby.

Amber, needing a fix was the first to ask, "What are we doing here Logan? And if it's what I think it is I'll need my own room."

Laughing, Logan O'Lakes replied, "Easy friend, we are here to rest and if you think I'm buying rooms for a bunch of trashcans you have another thing coming. Just act natural, in the morning I'll clean you out then we'll move on. After parking the truck and reassuring Amber that staying in the van was the best option for both herself and Hayden, Logan made a bee line for the inside of the hotel lobby.

Walking up to the counter an aura of pot mixed with coffee burning filled the air. To the left was an abandoned carafe of coffee from years ago that dried-out then turned black from the constant heat. Next to the forgotten joe sat a few pastries that very well could have been from the 70s by the design on their outer packaging.

From there, the faded yellow walls still did what could be done to express some sort of flower pattern that hugs the room with its vintage furniture. Green and blue mixed with tables that face chairs all covered in a vinyl wood that resembled an abused spouse.

Ding! The front counter bell pulled Logan back towards the receptionist desk, holding a stoned overnighter in some sort of polo jumpsuit tied in the middle with a Windsor knot. The latter was adorned with images of chickens on it that used to be red to match the jumpsuit. Staring at the wardrobe just a little too long, the night keeper spoke up out of their fog, "Like it? The gentleman's tie was my old man's and well, this polo thing is just comfortable. Are they not the cutest combo you have ever seen together? How lucky am I that my old man worked at a chicken restaurant and this jumper showed up in my neighbor's trash?"

Logan with some difficulty responding as the only people he had talked to in months were trash cans, replied, "Well, I suppose the odds were in your favor." Hungry with a sense of delirium went on.

"So, there is a chicken place around here?" Tightening her belt as some sort of chicken ninja, a laughter followed.

"Oh heck no. The old man sold his chicken restaurant years ago to some younger person who went by Saddie Tarous. The old man bought a plane and moved away and well, Saddie here ran the entire bird empire into the ground just before disappearing. My old man came back to try and save it but unfortunately, before they closed Robbie's, the name of the location, the fryer exploded one night."

Looking down while playing with the time, "this is the only piece of him that was found at after the accident. Even his car disappeared in the great fire. Anyway, enough of the jawing. What can I get you and how long do you need the room?"

Chuckling, Logan replied empathetically, "All night with one bed if you can manage."

With a few clicks a bedroom key was produced along with the receipt that was accompanied by tiny smiles. Turning away, Logan could feel the sorrow still fighting over the words that the conversation held. Hesitating with a deep breath he added, "You know what, it's been some time since I've had a conversation not with trash cans. If you get bored, why don't you come join me? I think there are still some snacks in my travel bag that might make for an interesting dinner."

Chicken Girl smiled, "Maybe I will bring my lunch up within an hour or so and we can split my sandwich."

With the air around the two of them a little more positive than before Logan now felt comfortable leaving the lobby to make the transition from outside light on the inside. It didn't matter if she called or not but the thought of her actually joining him for a 3:30 a.m dinner fluttered around until there was nothing else to think about let alone the trashcans sitting in the haul it yourself cab just outside. How angry would Amber be if she only knew what was going on without her consent.

With that said, once Logan reached his room he took the two visible trashcans and placed them in the closet with the safe next to the ironing board. He could not take any risk of them telling Amber about this mystery guest if there would happen to be one.

A few episodes of reruns went by until there was a point the eyelids started to give in to the objective of sleep. This was betrayal to the Chicken Girl but understandable as the drive and been 45 minutes past bedtime, sleep seemed more reasonable. Frogs began the dream and in a moment before too late the door shuttered with a knock.

"Housekeeping!" yelled The Voice. Startled, Logan awoke. "Home-keeping," bang, bang, bang, rang the door vibrating all of its parts. Still slightly in a nod Logan walked over to look through the hole in the door where a peep hole had once been installed. Through one side the soda cleaner started losing their temper that matched how well they wore their clothing. Again, bang, bang, bang, tossing the door to hit Logan on the head as he jumps slightly backward from the obvious attack. "This is housekeeping. Let me in or I'll use my master key!"

Unlatching the swivel lock then the deadbolt Logan opened the door to greet housekeeping in his boxers with eyes full of swollen hopes of sleep. Pointed, Logan started, "Yes, yes, I see that you resemble a housekeeper or almost one, how may I help you?"

Taken back, the older person looked around as if to be lost in a room with no lights. Stumbling a little then returning to save the situation the cleaner replied, "Robbie? Robbie is that you? Please tell me that is you."

Confused, Logan looked closer into the moment to realize that the employee was in fact blind. Feeling the silence, the housekeeper turned to the next available door in the hotel hallway then paused, kissed a gold necklace around their neck, then knocked, yelling, "Housekeeping!" Bang, bang, bang, bang, "I said housekeeping!"

With no answer they continued down the hall with no response, besides a few vulgar words that landed on a never swaying hopeful mind. Not sure who Mark was or the relationship to the cleaner he had, Logan returned to the bedside. With only a few breaths between moments the phone rang and within one pulse Logan answered the phone as if it were some sort of call from the Sargent ordering an air raid to save the people on the ground from an ambush, "Hello, this is Logan."

"Hey Logan, this is the Chicken Girl from downstairs. Are you still available for lunch? I know it's late but my time got lost following a mouse around the kitchen.

If I don't set it free tonight the manager will capture it for next month's convention, then serve it as sausage to the unlucky that stay here. Oh, by the way I'm obligated to tell you that we do serve a complimentary breakfast from 6 a.m. to 6:30 a.m. after that we lock everything back up to save it for the next day but there will be some sort of coffee available."

Sluggish, in an attempt to smile Logan returned, "I'm a late sleeper so that's okay. To answer your question, yes, I'm awake and would enjoy your company if you still wanted to split our rations."

With excitement in her voice that you can grow anticipation on, Chicken Girl went on, "Great, I'll grab my lunch box and be right up to your room. Just make sure the TV is off. You know that they watch us from that digital window, right?"

Laughing, Logan agreed, "No TV then. Great, I've crossed out my *be right back* sign to say, *go somewhere else* so we won't be disturbed." Followed by a gritty chuckle, both blushing over the phone but feeling like the redness was mutual, two ends hung up. It's been years since Logan or

Chicken Girl had spent any time away from the homes they cared about.

Amber, Hayden and the trash cans were all growing a little restless of the crypt that they had to live through for the night. Opening the curtain of the hotel room, Logan could see smoke blowing from the side of the truck Amber was sitting on, thinking to himself that she should really quit those things. In the driver seat Hayden was curled up in aspiration to find fresh air that resembled the driveway that was so many miles away at this point. All three far from home missing the tradition of a life that once made sense.

Trash was produced, went out, then was picked up. A few days ago, everything was simple. Now, they had a truck of illegal prisoners being hauled off to a location in shared silence. Not to mention Chicken Girl was on her way to talk. An actual human, ready and willing to talk. Logan took a second to freak out in a controlled manner involving rational behavior of taking a few pharm pills from a deceased neighbor's yard remains. Shaved even, a little knock hit the door.

Soon a second knock followed the first with a final soft dollop of, "hello?" Logan felt the air thicken to the point it hurt like he was breathing in tiny ice cubes. One second left before he reached the door his face swelled pushing fresh clothing over it and teeth into a smile that ended with a saluting of the hair. Unlocking the gate with mild retreat, turning the faux golden doorknob, the sheer and shy presence of the Chicken Girl appeared.

Far behind etiquette, "Hi, Hello, Chicken Girl," both greeting one another for several moments. The house cleaner passed the situation making chicken noises only to continue to cluck all the way down the hall then disappear into an elevator.

"Why don't you come in," moving aside Logan pointed the way in words as to offer direction towards the Chicken Girl she had never considered before. Watching her pass was like a rainbow in the mind of Logan that could not have an ending but if there was it would definitely be there.

Walking past Logan, Chicken Girl skipped the table and chairs to find a comfortable spot in the middle of the undressed bed. "Hope this is okay Logan, those chairs are really just uncomfortable."

Smiling, "Perfectly okay with me." Returning the locks to their secure location Logan slouches over to his bag and unfolds a grocery store plastic containment full of snacks from inside. Turning, he softly joined the Chicken Girl in the middle of the bed. Both now staring at each other, holding bags full of early morning lunch.

"Well then, I'll show you mine if you show me yours?" Laughing slightly while trying to stay cool the two started to expose their food treasures from inside the bags. Chicken Girl had a chicken sandwich cut in two and Logan had a half bag of beef jerky, chicken flavored chips and two tiny bottles of wine. Splitting up the goods onto napkins the best way that neither favored one or the other, all was set.

Logan thought aloud first after finishing a bite of sandwich, "So, you have to tell me about the housekeeper? Is it normal for her to roam the halls at night looking for a someone named Robbie?"

Chicken Girl rolls her eyes while gesturing that she was still trying to swallow a bite of jerky. Once consumed she replied, "You see, that's my mother, the owner of this hotel. Both my dad and brother were named Robbie. The day we received the news my brother did not make it back from Iraq, my dad decided to leave with one of the guests in her mobile home. That spontaneous action raised out of sadness would be the last dumb thing he did because that woman with the mobile home was a serial killer. Few weeks after we buried what was left of my brother, we barely saw even less of what was left of my dad. So, Cynthia, my mom now roams the halls for both of them. She completely lost her mind with Alzheimer's through extreme grief.

Oddly enough when all of this happened the elevator broke too. That's where mother now lives. In the elevator, just down the hall. If you push the up arrow the door will open, then close but go nowhere. It's a small dwelling but Cynthia swears that when Robbie comes back, she wants to be the first to know. Day in and day out, she sits in the elevator waiting until night when all the guests have arrived. At midnight she will make her rounds checking to make sure neither one took the stairs to a room as to not wake her. In her mind they were courteous like that. In fact, to this day they are both saints in her opinion. You know beside all the cheating and stealing they did during their time here."

Finishing the tiny container of wine Chicken Girl sat back on the bed, quickly changing her smile to sadness then back to some sort of middle compromise that usually ends with a bad decision. "Done with your food Logan? Because if you are, we only have a few more minutes to get naked before my break ends."

Leaning back himself while looking directly into the Chicken Girl's eyes, "Wait, I thought your family owns the place?"

"We do Logan, but someone has to ensure my mother's future of living in the elevators. Do you know how hard it is to find lift space for rent? Not to mention they are always in the worst parts of town. Regardless, my buzz is wearing off and I only orgasm high." Chicken Girl then rolled off the bed, hung up her chicken tie on the lamp and unzipped her jumper. There on her back was a tattoo of a rooster standing on a tiny moon looking Upward at a red planet that might have been Mars.

Just before Logan went for his belt a car horn went off that was on a date with some family man yelling, "Hello, hello, is anyone here? I'm tired and need a room now! Chicken Girl, where the hell are you?"

Turning while zipping back up she grabbed her tie and stopped long enough to say she was sorry through her eyes, then left with a few simple words still hanging between them, "Make sure you lock up behind me, my mom is also a little handsy." Slam, the hotel door closed.

Logan finished the night fully clothed, thinking about what could have been if Chicken Girl was not a hotel owner and he had more friends outside of the trash cans that surrounded his life.

The next morning, he took the receptacles out of the closet to fill them full of the late lunch leftovers. Making a somber way down the stairs into the lobby to return the key, with hope that his date would be there. Instead of a pretty face, a man sat behind the counter looking confused as to who Logan was let alone what he was doing with a key.

Logan broke the moment, "Good morning, just returning my room key."

"Who the hell are you? I did not check you into my hotel. Are you homeless? I'm calling the police."

"Stop," Logan spouted in rebuttal, "wait, yikes hold on, the Chicken Girl checked me in last night. You know, red jumpsuit with a chicken belt, the owner?"

The man behind the counter just kept shaking his head with his chin tilted upwards, "Drugs, you're on drugs, aren't you? Just look at that outfit with one backpack to make up your tall tale of trespassing."

"Seriously," Logan continued, "I came in late last night around 1:00, maybe midnight and some girl check me in. How do you explain the key card?" Logan stood there holding a gift card from the chicken restaurant down the street in the air. Both let their eyes dilate in effort to digest seriousness matter that now held them both captive. In a moment like this, time could get ugly or just continue.

In this case the desk clerk sat down out of exhaustion, "Did you trash the room and can you pay for your stay?"

Relieved now, "No and absolutely, yes."

"Okay," continued the owner, "you're lucky it's Sunday and the moment just before I had your truck towed from my parking lot. Oh, and there is an extra fee to park in the hotel parking lot." Some electric cash went through the air as if nothing happened.

Walking back to the moving van, Amber looked at Logan with a cigarette still billowing wildly, "Long night?"

Logan, "Yeah, I guess you could say it was a night of chicken."

Hayden perked up after hearing in Logan's voice, "Who won?"

"Probably the unbelievable, but we'll leave that for the security cameras to determine. As far as we go, we have a mission that is time sensitive."

Confused, Amber leaned in with a, "How so?"

"Nothing to worry about you two," said Logan with a loving demeanor, "let's get these captives to their new home." Amber and Hayden scooted over as their human friend joined them with his place behind the steering wheel. The engine of the truck moans to life then jerks into drive.

A little down the road Hayden remarked, "Why don't you look at that?" Fire trucks surrounded a local chicken restaurant. A girl in red stood outside waving as they drove by. Feeling a little better knowing that he did not make up the entire night in his head, Logan took a deep breath and found a comfortable position. The drive was going to be short but still long enough to allow worry to fill his head if the Chicken Girl was just a figment of the lonely imagination of a photographer.

The only question remaining was about the mother who lived in the elevator. If he did make her up, did the chicken girl just go along with it? Was she crazy enough to care or simply enjoy the story that there was reason to be second-guessing movements in the night? Either way she was real. Oh, who really knows?

Logan was able to convince himself to keep on with the mission in striving to stabilize a role in society. No one has known the truth since the start of time, so no one has to know the truth about him. Reassured, he looked over to Amber and Hayden talking about something important enough that they kept the volume of their voice low, "Speak up you two, what is it?"

Amber looked at Hayden then Hayden looked at Amber and she looked over to Logan. "Oh, you know, just talking again, that's all."

With a glare mixed with salt and lime Logan returned an, 'I'm used to it,' look that also forced a confession. Hayden shifted then replied, "Well, you know, there are a lot of cans back there. What if they attack us when we open the door? Even worse, what if they go to the authorities? The sanitation department might not be so understanding about the transportation of unregistered trash cans. Let alone ones that we plan on dumping off at a random location.

We just think it might be best to really nail down a plan of action. All it would take is for one trash truck to see us for this entire operation to stink. Not to mention, how do we know that one of the captives will not run off to tattle on us? Logan, they've seen our faces. They know what we look like. Maybe, maybe there's better solution."

"Oh, for heck's sake Hayden. Logan, just pull over," replied Amber, smoking her cigarette down to the filter then tossing it out of cracked window. "Look Logan, what Hayden is trying to say is that we think it might be best if we just recycle the bastards or toss them off a cliff into the ocean. You know, whatever the next few exits have the offer. Are we really morally obligated to save them? After all, you did have the cans caged and left for dead in your car closet. Let's just finish what you started. Let's take out the trash cans to the curb." Tapping a last cigarette out of the carton, Amber let what she said resonate while she started a fresh burn.

Breaking the silence once again, she followed up with, "Not to mention, we need gas and cigarettes. So, let's stop and think this all over but more importantly let's get more smokes." Slightly fearful of Amber when she does not have enough peaceful nicotine in her, Logan looks for the next exit that had a gas station that carried her brand. They had not been on the road for a long at this point, but they did need gas.

Hayden twitched a little out of the seriousness of the conversation then added, "As long as we're stopping, I would like one of those space drinks in a can, 'sex on the beach,' I believe they're called."

Both Logan and Amber had a question. Logan spoke, "Since when do you drink Hayden?"

"Well," he replied, "Since when did we talk about driving entire trucks of innocent cans to their death? Things are about to change and if you want my help, I'm going to need something to kill my conscious, possibly even my soul." Amber offered Hayden a cigarette and he declined. "A can is recyclable Amber, those filters are not."

With a little sense of pity hanging around the truck cabin like low-hanging fruit and eggs, it appeared. Anticipating a turn signal, the three of them along with a truckload of prisoners headed to the Quick Stop. With a squeak of the brakes the crew arrived at pump number three. "Okay then," said Logan, "one pack of Lucky Strikes for Amber and one can of bravery for Hayden."

Hayden, offended, "Hey now, why is Amber's vice okay but my needs are worth insulting?"

Amber put out her last cig and tossed it out of the window onto the ground of the gas station. All three waited for an explosion that never happened. Chuckling, "because Hayden you're fearful but I just don't care."

At that Logan shook his head, cracking the window for Hayden and Amber, then headed inside.

The person at the next pump yelled over, "Hey! You can't leave it like that."

"I cracked the window for them," replied Logan in a questionable manner.

"No dude, you can't just leave your truck running."
Returning specially to the moment, Logan thanks The
Stranger then turned off the truck, locking the door and
returning to the original trajectory towards the cashier.
Logan can hear The Stranger asking his wife if she thought
there were dogs in a hot van that was now turned off with
no AC.

Her voice cracked a little when she said, "Just take
a look when he's inside and if he does, call the cops and
you can break his windows with our freedom bat."

The Stranger, a bit of a hulk was nodding out of
agreement as Logan watched their reflections in the gas
station window. Unlucky for them, Logan thought, Amber
needs her fix, get ready to be yelled at for snooping.

Ding, the door made a sound to announce Logan's
entrance into the gas station. "Hello, welcome to Quick
Stop," repeated, a voice that felt half-dead connected to an
obese individual with high blood pressure.

Not interested, Logan just made his way to the
coolers for a few items that ended with the dreaded
descent to the registers where the greeter had been the
entire time looking down on their phone. Reassured that

their mask was around their neck, Logan looked up into the cashier's eyes, "Hello, I would like a pack of Lucky Strikes as well."

Grunting, wiping the top of their head then ringing out the entirety of items being purchased, handed Logan a receipt. They took a phone back out of their back pocket while repeating, "Thank you for shopping at Quick Stop." Afterwards, a meme about the stupidity of others came across their screen and with that Logan collected the bag to return outside.

Opening the door, he could see The Stranger pulling on the handle of his truck while whistling for the imaginary dog he wished to save from two minutes of eighty degree weather. Honk! His wife warned him that I was approaching and with that he scuttled off. And people think I'm insane, Logan thought to himself. Unlocking the truck door Logan tossed the smokes to Amber while handing the alcohol drink to Hayden. In a form of self-love, Logan cracked open a bottle of water from Maine.

Amber pointed out, "You're forgetting one thing Logan, gas you dumb Irishman." With a grudge, gas was pumped into the truck all the sounds of restlessness prisoners tapped on the walls of their confinement.

The Stranger next to him just stared as if they too could hear the cries from within the truck. Stressed, tapping his left foot as if that would make the pump run faster, Logan began to worry. If we have the cops called on us now, we will never make it to following any of our plans. What would the Sanitation Authority do to a person with this many unregistered waste bins? He looked over to catch the woman on the phone, while her husband pretended to check the engine on their electrical car.

Click, the pump topped off. Oh, thank goodness, all I need is a receipt and then we can get out of here. If only Amber and Hayden were not so needy, we could have avoided all of this. Breathing deeply in an attempt to stay cool, the pump beeps. A message read, please see cashier for receipt. Great, this could have been used on my taxes but forget it. There is too much attention on us already. We need to be on our way.

Returning to the cab, Amber and Hayden said together, "Logan the cops are here," and, "in numbers." Before Logan could respond, a police car pulled behind and in front of the box truck. Two other law enforcement vehicles block the entrance and exit just in case the moment sparks creativity.

Hayden cracked open the drink only to toss it down in one gulp. Amber lit a cigarette and said out loud with a glimmer of hope, "Personally I hope they rough me up a little. I've always been into that kind of danger. Breathing heavily while the light grew brighter, the fogged glass held back a crowd of watchers, who started to verbally unload without knowing any truths.

One man said, "I heard he is a bank robber," while a woman replied, "No you fool, that's the famous Hollywood guy that supposedly hung himself."

Another said, "No, no, no he is the inconsiderate jerk who left his dogs in a hot truck cab while he enjoyed himself in the cool air at the gas station to buy beef jerky."

The banter continued until the cops had exited their cars then went over to the crowd to disperse the unsafe gathering. In a moment, the only two left were the ones that had called in the issue. A man by the name of Sergeant Charlie Strokes wrote down what the accusers had to say in a small yellow notebook. Thanking them, he turned to face the truck. Walking over, with one hand on a gun and the other clicking a pen it was clear that this particular individual could multitask. You know, the type that chew gum and walk at the same time. This cop could shoot with his left then write a report with his right.

Regardless, Logan stayed cool while rolling down the driver window in effort to welcome the obvious conversation that was about to happen. Opening first to establish a sense of control, Sergeant Strokes spoke. "Good evening there, would you please put your hands on the steering wheel." Logan did so. "Great, now would you please tell me why I am here?"

Logan paused, "Probably because of those two over there with nothing better to do than to keep an artist on his way to a show."

Sergeant Strokes finished by walking up two feet short of the truck, "If it's okay with you, we are going to open the door now."

"We?" Found the air as Logan sat wondering if Strokes also carried some sort of communication with inanimate objects.

"Yes, you and me." Strokes commanded.

That making a little more sense, he agreed, "Okay." With a slight pull, the door opened, revealing the human and two trash cans all buckled in.

After seeing how empty the cab was the officer went on, "Now, I'm only going to ask this once, then a few more times in a more confusing way so I can catch you by tricking you to confess. Do you have anything illegal in the truck? Do you have anything illegal in your possession? Are you or were are you on your way to or from a location that consisted of anything illegal?"

Logan, with an open optimistic response, "Like an officer with a low sense of suspicion searching a man's vans without a warrant?" Both Logan and the officer knew that was the wrong thing to say. Quick to fix the situation Logan said again, "No."

"Then you won't mind stepping out of the vehicle slowly." Unbuckling, Logan stepped out ignoring Amber and Hayden's cries to just take off in a unique car chase that would end in a crash. Calmly, Logan stepped out then went to sit on the curb while the truck was searched for anything uncommon. Lucky for him, trash cans still did not have rights in this state.

Strokes walked over to where Logan was seated. "So, why do you have so many trash cans with two of them buckled in the front seat?"

"As you may know," Logan replied, "I'm a famous artist. Known for my work in photography as well as the human condition of throwing away items. All this is a statement now late to a museum."

Rubbing his jaw and thinking about his niece who is an artist, Strokes replied, "Do you teach kids?"

Struck in the heart by what he said, Logan replied in a defeated manner, "No."

Both disappointed, the officer handed Logan the keys to the truck. Still sitting he could hear the officer debunking the couple's claims that there were dogs in the car, The Stranger's wife arguing, "But look at him, he has to be up to no good." Only to be shot down by, "Ma'am he's an artist."

With all of that now aside, Logan return to the cabin of the truck to toss over the seat belt and hope Amber would have some positive words of encouragement to continue. "Well," said Hayden, a little drunk, "We got away from that so who's to say what else you could get away with. Maybe we should plan diabolical weekends more often. Dumping trash cans and like items could be our thing. Some assassins focus on politicians, celebrities, informants and whatever. We three could focus on those who really knew those people. The only ones close enough to see their trash firsthand. I can see it now. We hire maids to go into important people's homes then bam! We kidnap the kitchen bin along with the office bin. Thereafter Logan can question them and as soon as we gain their trust it's the shredder or recycling plant for them."

Amber turned to ignore the idea that very well was Logan's mental disease which gave him the power to talk to trash cans. No one would believe someone so different than himself. Shifting into drive, the van was once again making a plot down the road. After that there should not be any more required stops that had ordinary people attending to the location. In a way, the continued direction without a stop brought peace to all three travelers. From here, all they had to do was get along.

Hayden drunkenly played with the radio until the sobering tired him with the only solution being sleep. The low hum of the tires distracted between Amber chain-smoking with Logan overthinking the miles.

"So Amber, did you ever see our relationship taking such an adventure as this?"

"Haha, considering you never shared that you hoarded my kind, no. Logan, you're an odd individual who obviously has abandonment issues. That said, in the beginning when you captured me, I really hoped that you would grow out of the need to talk to us. More so Hayden. You know he looks up to you for direction? With all of this I'm a little worried that he might never be the recycle can he once was."

Taking a long drag that ended with words flowing out from underneath smoke, "Logan, we are trash cans and you are a human. We may never completely understand each other's role in this universe. It's true but we are both alive. Trash cans and humans can live together in harmony. We just have to want it."

Unsettled, Logan replied, "Do you want it?"

"Absolutely not. Until your kind has gone through the torture of my kind, we will never be equal. You have no idea what it's like to be the carrier of the waste that society generates. How could you possibly understand the lost pride that trash cans have undergone. At worst, people use trash talk regarding your direction. We literally carry the waste of humanity. Everything that you thought was not good enough for your pocket at the moment, ends up in our soul. I'm helping you to free the cans. After that, I just might be the one that rebels against you and your unthankful kind. People might have built this world but that does not mean this misuse of sanitation will continue.

We are strong, united and most importantly, needed. What would you do if there was no where you could dispose our own filth? Exactly. We would all be in a large pile of s***. Working together, is the only way but not until the people are torn down will they understand the daily struggle of trash cans. A true equality is on order even if it's the planet killing everything in hopes to save itself."

Thud, Logan ran over a raccoon while the receptacles in the back cried for help. Hayden woke up, "What was that?"

Amber leaning in, "Reality Hayden, simply reality." Unassured, Hayden passed back out while Amber waited for a rebuttal from Logan. One never arrived out of his own interest to house trash cans in order to meet whatever waste disposal needs came along.

What others had simply gone without, he had in abundance all that was practically forgotten about. Click, the radio came on under the direction of Logan's guilt. The song that came on the radio was helpful as a distraction from the static air, but the lyrics brought the potholes of the trip back into the subconscious.

Why was this trip helping to resolve years of misuse and lies? Only time, a lot more time, could fix the relationship Logan O'Lakes had formulated with his receptacles. With just the road and a smell of the occasional burnt cigarette the plan forward wandered further into the night to meet the moving van at the retirement home that now lay but an hour away.

When they were estimated to arrive, goodnight should have been around long enough for even those with too much pain to sleep to be occupying a bed like a chipped brick. With two more miles, the lights and their destination glowed on the horizon and with a sense of promise that this would all be over with wasted time as the sole victim.

Wobble, wobble, wobble. The truck on the passenger side was beginning to lift rapidly to the point Hayden and Amber started planking off one another. In the back of the truck, you could hear the younger trash cans start to cry as they awoke from a nap while the elders yelled out, "I'm seasick."

Hayden spoke with a tremble, "Um, why are we going up and down like your personality at the end of the month?" Amber laughed while shooting Logan a look that made this statement true.

Logan answered, "No idea, you two just hold on to each other we are almost there."

Amber looked at Hayden replying, "Keep your hands above my waist sir." Meanwhile, Logan tried going faster, slower, even slower, even faster, trying his best to find the optimal speed and bump ratio. Amber gave out a sigh feeling like the plan had felt this way the entire adventure. She tossed a smoking cigarette butt out the window only to be responded by a giant Bang!

The truck lifted into the air to land on a naked tire rim that quickly started to spark wildly after meeting the pavement. At this point the stealth approach had been compromised as the entire party was now screaming at sixty miles an hour and descending. A cloud of dust ended the moment with a sense of calm when the feeling of movement resided. In fact, all present were now silent. Completely silent. One by one the prisoners in the back started to whisper amongst themselves about the possibility of Logan's well-deserved death.

Popping out a small dent from her side with a large cough Amber informed the others about the situation. By the expressions that formed from the moaning all around Hayden was the only one slightly relieved that Logan was okay. "Well, that happened," said Amber, "Now what?"

Logan had already started to put on a pair of gloves while he responded with action, "It's just a flat tire. Wait here while I find the replacement so we can deliver these things and get home." Stumbling out of the cab onto the ground the air was cold with a giant greeting of nothingness. Logan was now in a deep distraction on if anyone heard the tire explode or if he remembered how to change one.

The only way to do it was to push through it he thought to himself. Now where is that spare? Meanwhile back in the cab, Amber and Hayden grew bored waiting for Logan while sleep came over eyes in the form of a dark night. It was not long before the entire truck fell into a dream, leaving Logan the only one stuck amongst the living on the edge of a side road that eventually descended to an old folks home.

Frustrated, Logan now sat in thought on the ground with his back to the bald. What a night this has been, first the cops and now this. Maybe it would be better to just leave all of them here and head home by myself. I really do not need this amount of distraction in my life right now. Between working on my next photo series, mixed with the craziness of the outside world, this really is too much. Not to mention the guilt building up inside of from treating these poor souls with no respect. No, we must continue.

Together, freedom will ring for those I've collected and I will finally listen to Amber's opinions. Standing up in a rush, Logan turned around quickly, tripping on his shoelace only to go head-first into the path of a passing trash truck. In about half time the truck took to stop, there was a streak of Logan O'Lakes a mile and a half long smeared onto the road. It looked like a bucket of red paint had fallen out of the back of someone's pickup truck. Not even his beard could be recognized.

In shock, Amber with Hayden jumped out of the truck in horror of what was in front of them. Hayden started to cry while Amber tried to hold back her emotions with a cigarette. All felt bleak for their human friend, continuously spread out into the other lane. Amber's heart was furious yet relieved about the possibility of leading a normal life. One where the family cared if she sat out in the rain or filled with sludge water. Slowly, hope came fast, even for Amber.

To make this situation even better, the driver from the trash truck was opening his door revealing a hunk of a man. Short with a belly, sporting a dirty baseball cap attached to a full head of hair blending in perfectly with a two foot long greasy beard. He slowly walked over to Amber and let words fall from a toothless mouth.

"Why, you are the prettiest can I have ever seen." Grabbing Amber in his arms, he leans her down on her rim to kiss her.

Slam! The loud noise of the moving van's driver door shook Amber and Hayden from their dreams. Logan sat smiling at the confused comrades, replying, "All fixed, let's get this heap of load holders to their final destination." The old diesel groans to cast out black smoke from the exhaust while the brake released gears ready to pull them off the side of the road towards success. "Amber, should we turn on the air? You look a little hot?"

Snarling back at Logan, "No, oh no. I'm just peachy that you are so freaking great." Caught off guard, the radio was turned back on to avoid any further exploration of that particular motion, surely attached to unpleasant circumstances.

Hayden was first to point out, "There it is Logan, your old folks home. And by the look of how many lights are on we are still the only ones awake."

"Then let us move fast before that changes." Logan assessed the situation, pulling around back of the building. The idea was just to line the prisoners up with the others already present. After all, they already had five bins sitting out, who would notice twenty or so more? With the truck's lights out, the heat wagon came to a squeaky stop before the engine silenced.

"Okay, remember the plan you two. Keep your mask on at all times and if any one can in the back starts yelling, stick this duct tape over their mouths and slightly give them a threatening look. Got it?"

"Sure thing, Logan," replied Amber with a sense of worry for the human. Hayden shook his head at the lunacy of all this.

"Great, let's move." One by one the trash cans were placed along the back of the building. "Bring the women and children first, leaving the elders for last."

So far, all the prisoners were silent and joyful that they no longer had to live in fear of Logan's tyranny. For them this was the day that would forever represent freedom for their people. Yes, this was the day that would be taught in trash schools all around the world. There will even be a holiday to commensurate the period following the Logan O'Lakes dictatorship. All of that was worth only a few more moments of silence. If this went well, he would drive off with only the traitors sitting in the cab and the exported bin family would never see the inside of another garage sale again.

Only a few more left before the wall would fall. With five trash cans to go, three trash cans to go, Logan picked up the second from the last with little care mixed with urgency. Turning to carry the tiny bathroom bin out of the truck the small blue prisoner with a grocery bag still hanging out of the edges bit Logan on the hand.

Smashing teeth together, he did everything possible to not make a sound. Now on the floor of the truck the little blue bin turned to face Logan man to can.

"So Logan, you think you can willy-nilly drop us off without any repercussions? What are we supposed to do, let you go back to your human life while never thinking about what was really going on here tonight? You bastard! You freak of human nature, you, you terrorist!

Because of you, I grew up in your garage. Never knowing what it was like to be fulfilled every week then empty like everything deserves to feel. Best years of my life were spent empty without even the smallest bit of trash to complete me. No, you cannot get away with this in the end because I stand for freedom!"

Logan, in shock of this rather unnecessary testimony reaches out for the duct tape but is too slow. The little blue bin lets out a yell that sounds more like the honking of a car horn. Once out of breath, all stood there waiting for something more to happen. It didn't, so the little trash can yelled again. Nothing. Again, again and again until out of breath, the radical had to sit down.

Feeling sorry for the little guy, Logan went over and sat down next to the enemy. Both now perched on the tailgate looking up at the stars. After some time, Logan offered an olive branch, "Is there something you want to talk about?"

"With you Logan, never," came in reply, hopping off the truck to the ground as an elder woman rounded the corner of the truck to find a little blue bin standing there.

She cooed, "Oh, how cute, a blue trash can!"

Replying, "How cute, an old woman."

In fright, the senior cried out, "A talking trash can!" Then proceeded to kick the little blue bin through the air right into an empty larger can.

Relieved from the extraction, she then turned to Logan to say, "Did you see that?"

"Yeah, you have to forgive the attitude, these trash cans, they are rescues and you know how they can be."

Both acknowledging how rescues could be mean, the elder woman joined Logan on the tailgate, "So, you talk to trash cans too sonny?" she asked him. "Yeah, always have, probably always will." Replied Logan.

"Me too," she began, "No matter the medication they stick me on, they always find a way to communicate. For a while in my youth, I kept it a secret but after my partner died it was nice to be able to go to the hardware store and buy new friends.

Oh, the conversations we would have about all the exotic places they were made. It's because of them I got to travel the world vicariously. Now, don't get me wrong there have been some nasty ones like that blue fella but overall, this gift is a blessing.

Once a few years back my kids caught me talking to Rodney. He was a great can built in the 1950s. We did it all through the years but that's over now. My kids walked in one day on us sharing a spaghetti dinner. A few days later, I'm here."

In an act of understanding, Logan was pleased to offer, "Well, if it makes you feel any better, I have just dropped off a bunch more cans."

Trying to shine a flashlight along the back wall, a voice bristled, "Stop! You, the older woman."

Quietly, "Hey, shine your light over there." Slowly aiming the light back around, a barrel exited the cab garage that had not uttered a sound for years. "Rodney?" Spoke the woman, "Rodney, is that really you?"

Waddling over to the can placing wrinkled hands on the large rim with a shuffle, "Hello," the sandy voice listed upward to dark brown eyes. Coughing, clearing a forgotten voice, Rodney spoke, "Sue?"

"Rodney it is you! Oh, my goodness it's my old trash can."

Smiling back at Logan with a reply, "Thank you stranger, you have made my night." Returning to Rodney with a clenched fist she slammed the side of the can.

"You have been a bad boy, Rodney. Leaving me here alone. Just wait until tomorrow. First light I'm going to find a stick and put you back in your place."

"Sue, darling, wouldn't you rather torture a different can? Look at all of them." The other cans shuttered doing their best to not make a peep.

"You mean to say Rodney, that they all speak? Well, one can was fun but all of you. Just think of the games we will play." Chuckling a little to herself she walked the line of prisoners while giving a speech with hands placed behind her back, "I don't care where you originated from or who you might think you are, but this is my arena. If there is as much as one piece of trash out of place, all of you will be personally punished!

Truthfully, my medications leave me a little angry anyway so be prepared to provide me monthly offerings from amongst yourselves. If you fail to do so I will pick the poor soul to torture myself and they will never recover!"

Now laughing out loud, Sue turns to face the light from the flashlight to brag, "Was I convincing Rodney?"

"Oh, my I love," Rodney encouraged seductively, "You've always been a fantastical actress. Drag me back into your room, I can't wait to hear about the last thirty years of your life."

"Oh, oh Rodney! You salty trash can." Sue took Rodney in hand to walk to the end of the building before disappearing through the service door.

Amber and Hayden were now standing with Logan at the back of the truck trying to comprehend what just happened. Amber spoke first, "Was that weird for anyone else?" Hayden replied, "Creepy, absolutely creepy."

"Well, we can't judge," Logan offered in defense, "If it's true love, then who cares what they look like? You and Amber are cans, but I still love you."

Both feeling a little sick after hearing that line of words out loud, those aside Logan returned to what they had to do. "Okay," said Logan, "They're all free, except you two. So, with that, here is your chance to be with the others like yourself. Go find your own way in this world. Whatever you do though, don't talk to Sue."

Smiling, Logan looked at the tempted faces of disposal among his friends. All three stood around for many breaths of indecision. Sure, it would be nice for Logan to be free of this obsession, circumstances would be even more suitable for Hayden and Amber to live out what they're used to with others representing a particular round shape. The book might be a little healthier if this moment was a splitting.

Biting his lip, Logan went on encouraging his companions, "Really, I'll be fine. It's a big world out there for an artist and not having to come home to check on the trash might not be such a bad thing. At least here you will have someone take you out weekly in a perfect routine. With me, who knows. It could be a month before I remember your needs over my own. Also, the trash here is probably better. Mostly pudding cups mixed with other small containers that used to hold fruit. Back home, you know, our expendables tend to get weird."

Amber looked at Hayden then at Logan with a burning cigarette stuck firmly between two hardened lips, "Yeah, it'll be nice to retire but when it's all said and tossed, we need you as much as you need us. Who is going to talk you down next time you think it's possible to talk to anything else other than us? Come on, let's get in the truck. We have some planning to do before your next exhibit."

"Really?" Came hopeful surprise from Logan, "This looks like paradise for you two?"

Hayden mused the idea, "Most likely but by the looks of that giant dumpster they don't recycle here so I would be obsolete, probably having to repurpose something awful, like medical waste."

"Haha, don't feel too proud, they have specialized cans for that Hayden. Your only hope would come in the form of a compost container. At least that's Earth friendly." Both Hayden and Amber share a familiar look of distain at the comment.

"Okay Logan," Amber continued, "The truth is, passing this task onto another is something I'd hate. You know I don't like it when other people hang your artwork on the wall without me. Your pictures demand an obscurity that only comes from my unique understanding of your situation. Come on Hayden, let's get in the truck before we are left out with these common cans."

From there, all three climb back into the cab completely forgetting about the last trash can still in the cargo hold. "We closed the back, right?" asked Logan. "Oh yeah," replied Amber, "Hayden did while that lady was going off the deep end. We thought we might have to make a trash run for it and get out of there"

"Great," said Logan, "Let's get home where everything make sense and we can talk in private about the new year." The rest of the ride was spent posing different scenarios of Rodney and Sue, with a play on the other cans. Laughter filled the car without the use of the radio. There was this great relief that overcame the three of them, all now able to move on in a more focused way towards otherwise impossible goals. The only agenda now is to get Logan's prints to the gallery.

Meanwhile, in the back of the moving van sat one lonely can that had been completely forgotten about. All gray with a black pattern, it's easy to see why no one noticed the one foot high receptacle stuck in the corner.

As the truck hit a large pothole, the trash can went airborne, landing on its side then proceeded to slide around on its belly in a manner that represented a penguin gliding over ice. A heavy sleeper, it was only when this abandoned can smashed against the wall did she awake from a dream about being a comb. Startled, green eyes opened to meet the darkness of an empty truck. Quickly finding a sturdy base the little trooper wedged a small rim that surrounded her body under a loading strap.

"I can't understand this," she whispered in a way only herself would hear, "Where did the others get off to without me? Why did my family not realize that they were minus one? Who is responsible and could it be me? What could I have done to be the last?" Too afraid to push more emotion out in the shape of questions, the remaining being sang a little song her mom taught her at the factory before they were separated by size.

Big dreams, little room
A little you, so plastic, so true
You will be why, everywhere you go looks new
Every home will only have a few
Pretty trash cans, just like you

Rocking back and forth singing the simple tune for comfort until the hours proved too long in the battle to rejoin her dreams. That morning a middle-aged them opened the door of the moving truck and found the bin wedged in the corner in a neglected state.

Resting their corn broom on the side of the truck they picked up the little bin and proclaimed, "Perfect! You will be great in my kid's bathroom."

Trying to hold back the excitement the bin whispered, "Thank you," and in return they received, "You're welcome."

Before this tiny survivor could kill any more abandonment, she was buckled into the back of the station wagon on route to a new home. All she could do was picture how much fun it would be to belong to a young person full of imagination. The games they would play, the napkins full of makeup they would toss her direction. Oh, just watching them grow was going to be such a treat. A child and their trashcan, life could not be any sweeter.

Upon arrival the middle-aged them yelled out the window as the patter of little feet ran up to the car to greet their parent. "Hey love bug, how was your day of exploration and conquering?"

"Oh mom, you know, out of this world, duh!" responded the youngster with glee.

Giggling, Mom got out and went around to the side of the car where the forgotten vessel was sitting.

"I have something for you love bug," said Mom, opening the door as the little one's eyes lit up, "It's your very own trash can."

"Oh Mom!" Unbuckling the freeloader, the child declared, "This is not a trash can but a secret chest for all of my treasures." Clenched in the arms of her savior the two went inside to only start the greatest story of all time. A young friend that was no longer nameless, Joan and the secret chest would grow old together, eventually leading to Joan leaving it to Winter and inevitably little Betsy.

Chapter Five

Around The Trash Cans

With the truck back at the rental place and the three travelers resting from their time away from the mundane, everything was now in its place. Another day came but as for now it was time to reflect and be thankful for all that had happened. Unless you ended up with Sue.

After a long few days finding peace with sleep, Logan returned to the scene to address the previous crime. Meeting Amber and Hayden at the garage door, they both were excited to see how Logan would react to an empty car closet. Uncoiling a padlock, with a tug the door rolled open with ease. Inside was nothing but shapes in the dust where the prisoners used to sit. So, it was true. Logan really did drive them 100 miles away to an old folks home.

Then, looking back over to Amber and Hayden, only to notice two trash cans sitting by a property fence. No expression, Amber was not smoking cigarettes while Hayden resembled every recycling container you have ever seen. Lifeless, a face could not be seen between the two of them. Nervous, Logan turned back to the empty space while talking with the cans over a pulled shoulder. "It's okay, you don't have to say anything Amber, I know we should clean up the rest of the evidence.

Yes, Hayden, I'll move you, so the dust does not bother your allergies."

Silence. Sauntering over to Hayden, he pushed the can far away from the garage as not to get dust on it, with thought he reacquainted Amber next to him.

"Okay, I know you two don't like being that close to each other, but we have a lot to do without you both being in my ear."

An hour went by, three hours went by, then the day went over the passing of a week. Months traversed without a single narration from another trash can. Logan even let the trash build up in a battle to upset them but still no provocation was enough for them to speak. It was not being alone that brought the feeling of sorrow but lack of inspiration that had resided around taking out the trash.

Where there was once conversation, now existed perfect effectiveness. The challenge was gone. Where was the push back that once was delivered with a puff of smoke? No more guilt trips by Hayden about what was in the wrong can. At least at the end of most friendships there is a fret or a fight but here nothing offered itself up for clutching onto out of anger.

A bird hits a window and death is unstoppable, prompting a long walk from home and then the rain fell. Thinking, of a ship in outer space, with too far to go for a parachute to work. What once was a home of banter turned into a home of one. Yes, there are people out there willing to visit my time while fulfilling their overflowing need to expel conversation into each of my fissures but that seems even more lonely.

Left spinning on a chair at the desk with Hayden and Amber silent there was only one possible solution. Complete my next series of works for the gallery. Once done they would have to return to help me figure out descriptions, format, framing and as Amber promised, display. Yes, if I focus on the trash project then they will reappear as the confidants they've always been. Otherwise, what's the point? Amber and Hayden are the ones who came up with the idea of the trash series anyway. Without them this very well could be a disaster.

It's time to get back behind the shutter and share with the world what two trash cans showed me about the habits of how people talk about their garbage.

Rushing into the night, Logan spent the time needed to properly gather necessary equipment for the project. Wide angle lenses, night lenses but even more importantly, enough batteries to withstand a five-hour trek through the city. Nothing would be worse than to reach the limits of one's physical self to find the perfect pile of waste only to discover your power is exhausted. A water bottle, utility knife, bug repellent and plastic bags would also be stuffed amongst the equipment. Food along with mind suppressants would be brought along but in small supply as much would be found along the way.

With packing aside, only proper clothing and setting the date remained. With the night chosen for a few weeks out there was time to address the technical aspects of the exhibition. Such as the artist statement. This particular statement has haunted Logan for a moment, as the aspect of talking to trash cans seemed reckless with a side of endangering even for the creative sort. In so many words the time spent with Amber and Hayden had to be explained without actually acknowledging that he in fact spoke to them and at great lengths. Not just on the matters of photography but life too. Their round shaped confidence helped guide an otherwise mundane routine in promise to bring another successful day. In short, there was doubt this declaration could even be worth a mark without their inclusion.

Forget Hayden's uncanny ability to spell any word tossed at him. Amber was the perfect combination of sandpaper and salt that raised paragraphs like no other waste bin. The three were pillars on which a great triumph was built upon. Without support, there may only be an epic breach of ability. Partners, in this case acted as one, not merely an individual prevailing out of self-interest.

With reservation, Logan stood up to walk out the back door to confront the deserters one final time. Yelling, as if the level of the sound of his voice would benefit the situation while now awaking the neighbors.

"Trashcan? That is all you are now? Simple containers made to hold disregarded human waste for a week only to be tossed around the curb like a derelict foam cup, a common one if that. Look at you, this is what you are after everything we've been through? Ordinary receptacles in an average driveway waiting to be misused by your human? Here I thought the cans we took to the retirement home and gave up on were pathetic. We have come so far together, you pieces of trash!

I saved you from the dump, rescued you from becoming the very things you were built to hold. So much potential just vanished overnight with the retreat that doesn't even deserve an explanation. Nothing, that's what all this means to you, our friendship, nothing. Dear friends stuck in silence, that refuse to touch my ears with vibrations, betrayal knows this calloused hand well. If it's not from the worker, it must be from the traitor!"

With lowered eyes that did not hold a candle to loss of control, Logan continues in vain, "Don't say anything, as I thank you but definitely do not ever welcome you again. Congratulations Amber and Hayden, this final escapade has not only broken my empathy for the two of you but has only inspired a greater will to take the trash out in a way that will rot out your bottoms until rest proves to be the ultimate adversary of a burden's weight."

Lifting a small bag of trash from the kitchen, Logan tosses the junk into Amber while closing the lid on Hayden, turning his back to the scene, "We could have been more than this lost trio of broken homes. More than prison keepers of those who had nowhere to go anyway. Instead, you will be there and I will be here but stuck in a mobile state rather than stationary. Do not think this is easy or fair for either of us. As if anything is true, this of all things felt easy until it did not."

Closing the back door behind him only to open it slightly in hopes to hear a response, the passing cars instead promised another night of white noise. With the door locked, Logan crashed into a yellow chair. The item of comfort provided two cushions and happens to be in the kitchen as it was all there was. Living alone with two trash cans did not take much seating, let alone traditional placement of the seating.

That aside, the chaos brought his work closer to reality. The more like his world could be related to trash the better understanding there would be when it came time to shoot scenes of the neighbors' neglect.

Encompassed in the task at hand, the time became short when describing the death of Logan's willingness to lose his mind.

Chapter Six

The Artist Statement

With only a few days to spare before starting the hunt for tossed out moments worth capturing, Logan turns to pain in an undertaking to complete the very definition of his insanity in a way the world or at least investors would fall in hot tropic love with him.

Much easier if performed on the gallery floor, this endeavor forward was still exciting without inspiration from the symbols of sound printed on Styrofoam boards glued to walls in position with the art as art, such tags would be leaving most scenarios in a bunch of chaos for those inclined to read and view. Collectively, this statement was an ad. Separately, this draft of excuses lay the foundation of a text that would be examined by overcharged students with no future.

Regardless, here we are. Person versus paper in the challenge of a lifetime that ends with clarity. Well, a clear picture for those who need to understand what is being done in the photo and why. I stated the road that led here but never truly shared. Anyway, if this show is going to come together on time, a statement must be resurrected out of the nest with a healthy application of makeup to create desire. From there, Logan O'Lakes went over to the closet to find a working pen not far from paper and the determination required to begin his archaic process of writing the wishes of the wondrous founder in six lines of fictitious fun much the way a phantom visits those only watching free wine. Logan's statement came to light.

Exhibit: *Trashed*
Venue: Word Revolt Art Gallery
2023 to 2025
Snatched by: Logan O'Lakes

Artist Statement

Dear people of Earth, please receive this letter as my official resignation. From this moment on my time will be occupied by a longshot mixed with day naps. Thank you for understanding my decision to pursue other means of commentary. This time with you has been informative if not long enough. Your advice and direction has been anything but light. Still there is no harm in the concept that you pushed, just as long as those stuck in the hours are willing to be there with you. All aside, this adventure in the mundane has proven to highlight one common thread among all people despite their religion, faith, habits, or wealth. That common thread being trash.

No matter what neighborhood or car meanders down to every home in the country, it faces the same parable of art. Trash, trash cans, out front in some sort of container or left free like a yard ornament. Regardless, there it is. Our common concept. We all make waste. Now the interesting part. How do we dispose of that trash in front of our residence and in what manner? Is it stacked neatly or left resembling a car crash? Do we care how it looks as it is being there, a statement all its own? What emotion went into the action of dragging what was once suitable for inside, outside? We may never know but what if the windows couldn't repeat our exile?

In this collection of photographs, I tend to expose just that. The reason people talk about their trash in the manner that they do. Answering questions like, why does the trash look like it was tossed from a moving airplane?

Why do couches end up in pieces scattered, when only moments ago a family sat on it during a television hour? Why the chaos and do we not remember how to stack like sized items? Who died and left the lazy relative in charge of cleaning out the home? Who died and why should the neighbors care? Lastly, who owns that broken cabinet set and why wait until now to take them out?

Most of the questions above will be answered as a collective in a series of black-and-white photos. The images will be black and white in strategy to conceal a colorful narrative that implants judgment on folks when a few of their objects can be identified.

In conclusion, this collection of photographs printed on stock cream paper will encompass the real-life struggle of everyone when dealing with the task of tossing out the garbage of their life. Wasted or not, we all come to the point in life that leads us to face the simple act of tossing out a part or the actual thing we once bought. When that happens there is an emotion attached and this collection explores just that. Why are we so emotional when we toss out the items it felt good to buy? Could it be the loss or is it the memory of the moment that leads to the carelessness left curbside? With a snap the truth about why we toss out our household items in the fashion that we do will be revealed.

With that, I must ask you to hold off while this chapter ends and the garbage is delivered to the dumpster. Her name is Sheila but her voice has been silent ever since my trash has not been bagged.

*All of the art has been created using alternative methods.

Chapter Seven

Day 1: Harris Residence

Now that the dread was removed from figuring out an artist statement, the actual work of taking the pictures could begin. This was the part that made the most sense and what explained the most to those lost when wandering the halls of a gallery they heard about but have never been to. Like most, the art was a product only considered after advertising worked its lows.

Regardless, there is a time for standard fonts like there is a moment for a common discrepancy. We are not here to face the issues but to wage a psychological campaign on trash. After all, waste is alive and well. Living on every curve in all cities, around the world with no explanation as to why that debris was placed there and for what reason. Renting aside, Logan is about to start the evening of day one.

The ideal time to take pictures of people's trash was the night before pickup day. The darkness provided camouflage from those who would normally be awake during the day. Also, it was easier to focus on the topic without all the distraction of the backdrop. Logan was left with no choice but to sleep all day in effort to walk around all night. That and there was less sound to distract the moment inspiration came in the form of well tossed out bread. In a lonely way this alone time with the camera was also romantic and nature.

Both the camera and Logan wandering outside of the perimeter of normal function only to press faces together while experimenting with settings. Not to mention the secret use of lenses. All of this made even more exotic when there is a full moon or the hint of moisture in the air. Amber and Hayden used to poke fun about how close Logan was to his camera. Blaming their relationship on why he was single and would remain that way, never questioning the fact that he spoke to trash cans.

Regardless, they are gone now and this tiny portal capable of capturing time that represented current promotion was still providing comfort. With a fully charged battery, that feeling of companionship could last for hours if not all night. Shaking clear the roaming fog of the dark walk, Logan could see his first target just a few porch lights away.

The Harris residency with all of its abuse now sat vacant on the inside with a world of trouble left broken outside. You see, this particular home was a rental and with its prime location at the beach the rent was tremendous for the square footage. Perfect for an upper-middle-class bachelorette but impractical for the host of growing families that tried to live the dream and have more kids than bedrooms.

It seemed like every few months the home would fill with joy only to rot from the inside until the last reasonable action was to move closer to the city. Leaving Logan the perfect opportunity guaranteed to provide a glimpse into modern family life needing to file a prestigious dream related to location rather than weeks. It really is sad but in the end it's better to move on and stay together rather than splitting up out of splitting hairs.

Upon existence at the Harris home or the ex-home of the Harris family, it was clear who collected the most or was willing to give up the least. From the looks of the dry rot in plastic toys now faded from sitting abandoned and junk cars, it was clear the kids had lost the majority of the war. The stuff wore that is, evident from their boxes upon bins resembling a spilled trash can that a raccoon had just visited. It was hard to tell if the neighbors had carelessly ransacked the containers or if the banished residents just tossed out articles of clothing from their closet. The latter is probably accurate as some of the shirts and dresses hung tightly onto hangers still vibrant with color.

Also present was a pile of shoes ranging in gender from young to young adult and their condition seemed to be fair to good. They must not have planned on eating with kitchen utensils at their next location by the two large cooking pots full of knives dancing with forks that seemed to be looking at all the jealous spoons.

Not to bring up the coffee cups but out of the lack of displaced literature the sayings on the mugs are all that's left of this family's philosophical beliefs. Of course, there were some best parent generic cups mixed in with overpriced vacation relics that apparently are now forgettable memories.

Then there were words, sports, links and religion glasses that did not make the cut. Makes one wonder what mugs they did decide to take. Notwithstanding, one cup did stand out amongst the other stylish choices.

This chalice bared the mark, "Let's pretend I'm an engineer." Laughing a little to himself Logan was trying to figure out what type of engineer this particular person would like to pretend to be? Then as following most simple lines, the moment fell into being over complicated by trying to define what it actually meant to pretend.

Stepping on a photo helped the mind not to rant and exhumation continued with the mugs left to their fate except one, now tucked into a black bag next to the bottle of wine that was for a late drink in the nearby park.

Other items at this point started to appear as the time spent lingering grew longer, slowing to address the madness of a stranger's life. More intimate items like socks, underwear, diapers, and toiletries. All of which when put together made an excellent abstract photo of daily actions. Then there are the mattresses.

Oh, what a creative mind could conclude from the shape of a tossed out human body pillow. Everything from condition, size, quality, even location to the curb all told the true story about how someone existed inside their home. Not only that but how they existed in their private quarters. Impressions gave away if they slept alone, while well-aged spoke of their wealth and if they were lazy or not. How new the mattress was is important as well, older couples tend to keep them longer while divorced couples went through them as if the object directly represented the very person they were trying to get rid of.

In this case the Harris family tossed out the mattresses the kids outgrew. It's comforting to know that the parents still loved each other even through the hard times. Even if the kids are both bed-wetters. Leaving to question why they would pass out their pillows? Leave it or not, this is a rare item to find disregarded in the trash. Personal bed pillows seem to form a relationship with the mind they support in your dreams.

Not missing the rare moment to capture a used bed pillow, Logan snaps the photo in the manner like he had just caught something of great value when poaching in a distance forest. Not that he would kill an animal but it's the mannerism in this that is important.

Outside of that, old mail was scattered about with a few rough pens that occupied pencils that judged the few unused highlighters. Oddly enough, there was always a highlighter to be left behind. As an adult it's hard to picture the last time Logan used one but that did not stop the reappearance of them at every site, especially when it came to older people and their trash.

Listless of quickly pocketing other prescription bottles left in a plastic organizer, it was time to wrap up the photos at this location to seek unknown territory. The Harris home had been successful for many reasons but the trash led to a typical Sunday's wares. Sure, there was a lot of it but the confusion of how the items were tossed out did not leave much room for emotion. Logan was after objects that clearly had a journey from the inside to the outside that spoke a volume or two about themselves as well as the person rejecting the thing.

An item with a window into what had been given flight would be ideal. That is to say, stuff with so much baggage the occupant ground the crap out of line to be crossed in motion only to set it free towards the curb with no haste. Then, once the thing met its fate, relief resided in the constructed chaos that lay public. Victory in a Renaissance fashion that only could be brought upon the collective as an action against what the commanding human brought daily through owning tactile creations.

There's no desire for destruction but if pieces had
the form for the greater good in a photo, then so be the
person looking for freedom from broken promises. Taking
a deep breath Logan felt the pressure of splitting popular
rotations and had to stop before colder weather polluted
the craft and art was compromised due to personal
wondering. Breathing did not work, along side of thinking
about positive emotions like his time with Hayden and
Amber. Eyes closed, the right hand holding the time
machine started to summer.

With every heartbeat brought on by a darkness that
is better scraped from home, if only he was not in the
middle of a road well populated by better controlled
occupants, selectivity again manifested outwardly in the
lack of control his body had on the moment, leaving Logan
exposed to anyone that might be underway in observance
to his presence. Unconcealed but alone, the moon covered
with dark clouds was now lost in the meaning behind text
on creations, resignation meant going back.

Pulling the prescription out of his jean pocket that
was collected from the Harris home, Logan indulged in the
contents followed by a bee line for the park. Slowly, after

last time, that land of confusion on the curb of nonsense gave way to arrival as Logan opens his lungs to greet the dark, dry air. Thankfully he was alone, if not for a better word stranded by oneself that represented a column.

Strong hands with deep crevasses had bridges of hope, that no longer held a welcome sign offering a distant discount on what insanity was bought to today. First, as one person was experiencing it, Logan had calmed down. Enough to where the smell of laundry was detectable alongside the feeling of missing home. Breathing was hot, accountable and obtainable in a wok that fitted similar style of those now loose with their dogs. Exiting a tunnel, Logan O'Lakes returned to the now, with the kind of excitement that would follow any rescue mission. Shaking his head up and down to view what had happened while away, the camera sat presently awaiting the orders of its returning lover. So pleasant, it almost sounded like joy if items could feel such with humans.

Once fully back from the conversation with his camera Logan stood in boots still willing to hold legs. Vertical, the journey was resumed upon to capture the waste left in the shadows of a sleepy home. If not asleep, then residing and if not remaining, creating more content for the series crafted by those simply willing to let go. Forget and forgive was after all Logan's creative destiny as far as the oblivious aspect goes. Never mind below, Logan thought, if you're not looking for the high.

Shortly after the slow numbness wore off the Barrino home appeared out of nowhere like a mirage. With curtains constantly representing a bridge over a moat there is not much known about them besides the degree of severity of their privacy. It was said that they were bank robbers in the seventies hiding out from the world in an underground cavern beneath their home. Others assumed they were just too busy contacting aliens to be bothered by common folk like the neighbors. Logan's favorite though was the story about how they really did not exist but were a permanent art display acting out daily life as common people to make a point on the true absence of modern life.

Either way, these people always had the best trash. Rather it was today or next week they had a way of tossing out items that had no meaning to a home that knew what to begin with. For example, the TV they freed the other week. Yellow, covered in cigarette burns then left in mowed grass with a repaired antenna. The burns mocked the time that someone spent gambling on dog races then falling asleep to the evening news after losing most but winning some. Plastic yellow had been left to rot after a lifetime of partnership. So why now? Did they get a new TV or did the person who used this device just quit the addiction? If so, attendants have not received the signal in years let alone in 2020 from a TV built-in a time no one was a crook.

Along those lines they seem to enjoy tossing out lamps. Week after week, years after years, lamps would fall victim to the trash. Base, shade and all would sit properly reflecting often abandoned at the church. Only in this case there was the weather to think of, ruling in bold of hopes the sun would provide provocation for local kids to have an excuse to destroy what they could and not get in trouble for breaking.

Between the local youth and natural skies nothing was safe from rot, mold or decay, sitting in tow until structurally they disintegrate. Some patrons on the other hand had more of a military approach and just destroyed the item. Painful longevity compared to years of revolution seems imperative to a lamp but we are talking about ways of life. Regardless, all the items have fault whether in one format or the other. Cardboard, furniture, fabrics, plastics, leather, wood, vinyl, electronics and photos never to be found spring back from death when left in the heat.

Supposedly, being dumped by a human is the worst outcome for stuff the same way as being in love with someone who is in love with variety. It many ways it's probably the material you're made of mixed with how current of a lease anything has in the moment. Unfortunately, stuff as well as people go through the same rejection. Let's face it, beauty is passing while available opportunity constantly grows until silence. Extraction is a manner of survival for the living matter.

Come what may, Logan sees the next location for the feeling of hope to possibly ride a narrative that seeks to pull the poet out from hiding. Photography after all says what is needed without the implications of further dialect. Seriously, who cares about long conversations when just going to look can take you away? Joyful, Logan thinks of a few bad commercials that the, 'take you away,' saying was used, then wonders about how cliche he really is acting.

Happy in any terms with how his body feels, transformation from what was is now relieving. Something is finally working to balance the ego with the id and there are no complaints on either side. All that's left is to find the trash so long desired then do right by its final performance.

When all is said and done, this is just one big dive and we are as a group of spectators at best, failing to drive from high cliffs. There's no difference in feeling alone with or without a great space between us and them. In reality we are more like Them, These and even They, looking at us looking at them and trying it differently.

Tonight, the Bruno home looked as if a time traveler brought back a thrift shop and then quickly descended back to the store where they came from. Scattered in a fury laid plaid shirts mixed with records over broken cabinets covered in green wallpaper. A bike with what seems like a gas tank holding a flashlight pointed purposely towards direction from the 50s while slaking itself in a building milkshake from the rain on top of a map that showed possible outcomes for worming air patterns.

Mixed into the mayhem laid roller skates, slide projections of the national parks and stainless steel chairs from a navy base. All in otherwise good condition, something had happened here that had seen the outcome of a foolish range of possibilities. In truth, once Logan arrived, the lights behind the curtains went out in an unintentional oblige to provide the best backdrop darkness could offer. Satisfied with current provisions, Logan went on with his craft.

Pile #1 formed in a box of well used dog toys from the 60s. It was apparent this particular animal had been dead for years but the squeakers still worked, providing that this mouth was probably a female and not aggressive. Further digging would reveal dog tags of a dog that recognized the command of Willow. Other traces of the long tooth beast stop at that box.

Pile #2 confirmed alien suspicions to the photo album of 200 edified people touring the museum in Arizona near Area 51. Apparently, dogs are allowed and Willow was given a space toy to distract herself from the other visitors. Humans were offered a toy as well as way to award that they were old enough to go on vacations.

Pile #3 was a rebuilt castle of baseball cards. Wentworth's small inheritance now lies as useful as an index card in the library. If not used, still important but as far as the popular vote goes, not valuable. Sad, but in a cultural aspect trading our value for monster cards over humans make sense to our race. It's unfortunate that anyone wants to collect anything as if left alone stuff looks better without our interaction, leaving only the idea that is connected to a kite. Who is holding the string and why are we mad at the wind but not those producing the tether?

Pile #4 all three boxes of new highlighters, two boxes of pencils, seventeen pens and one container of five hundred paper clips. Red notepads mixed with white out bottles glare towards permanent markers minding their own company. Erasers made you see they had other objectives like making alliances with the soggy paper while observing thicker stock such as the folders more equipped to outlast droplets of any sort.

Bringing Logan back to the clear containers holding secrets. Some relics resided with common cleaning products of the body. Trends make cleaning hard for any venue let alone what's left after chasing a passion that is your identity. All that aside, Logan left empty with only a walk ahead to clear the mind tempted to break a peaceful scenario, otherwise drowning in need of a savior.

Hidden, tucked, camouflaged, and forgotten come as a relief. Picking a fruit, the apple lands juicy to lubricate the evening. Another score. Not as great as the first but better than the last. It's a wonder that people keep in their pockets to stop the truth of what really is going on around perfect mayhem.

Now collected, there is an impulse and guilt to return the items or not and the not wins out. Seriously, who cares about what item is never noticed. Between now and then it will be the then missed instead of the noun. That said, the Bruno house is full of questionable questions that terminate in a rough terrain. Simple is simplicity if only there were not great vibes that turn as rivers through sandstone. Logan, collecting what little is left wanders in a circle around what just happened.

Each house is not in tune with the opportunity of being a house. True homes. What? With what homes who? We eat the given with the granted eating us as a treasure. Stand as we, as an abbreviation until shorthand walks an

English mile. Say it or be said but do not fade as a sketch. Asphalt lays a perfect foundation until there is a pothole too large consume. Please stop me before it begins or we'll have another case of late-night roasting.

Secrets are discharged and all manners of creativity and indulgence end, dissipated with the simple gesture of a finger snap. After that, it should always remain the question? Who, if anyone, asked for the…... snap! Politics aside it's all what we are, it's not what we will be. Focus is on the trash, Hayden and Amber need us.

Back from another time, situations dream of a positive resemblance in a gate that is perfectly closed. Cold, strolling marks the otherwise thick pants worn by modern folk in style to divulge parts seen in past moments otherwise loved. Look no farther than to flash free from greatness in an attempt to understand bare legs. Naked in a manner to offset decisions, mocking for those who have already claimed freedom, in hindsight the revolution started in a collapsed manner. There is no recollection with an ability to destroy one over the other. Transgression is a tool used best in destroying the enemy or healing a wound to highlight this chapter. How are we not all blind?

All of the Amato Circle neighborhood was involved in a notion prompting the previous forty lines of text. Nonsense, caused by the picked drugs. The mysterious treasure found in an orange bottle had started to take its full effect while Logan now laid flat on the sidewalk blacked out from reality.

Cold, hard and slightly textured the bed beneath Logan felt like cement. Turns out, it was in fact concrete with the rising sun acting as an alarm clock over the horizon. Whatever had been concealed in the found pills did a number on this human capsule. Every once in a while, the misdirection of experience shakes loose the possibility that a substance might be stronger than they're represented color. Never an issue and always a concern after, Logan was not a stranger to waking up on a sidewalk bed. More so after a successful night of trash portraits.

Danger was part of the fun if the feeling of the unknown was not the exact purpose this project came to light or dark. There is a reason the people represented in the garbage cannot hold onto the life they built. Good times rather killed them, prolong the death, or made wondering a longer journey than just to the fridge and back. Regardless, without their pioneering of modern medicine there is not be the opportunity to take photos better left alone as a long conversation in the bar with too many lonely people making love to one drink.

Bones popping, the sudden now made a full recovery from the night. Still in a horizontal position the idea of returning to an upright height had never felt more useless if fear of being discovered was the driving factor. Not for the idea that people living in the neighborhood would not enjoy a random stranger camped out in a recovering body but this position might not have warranted evacuation.

Fortunately to the people, Logan knew human discretion gave way to unwarranted attention. The time to release the benefit of another day came faster than their reaction to the actual cause. With a rub of a shaved head mixed with the check of equipment the message was received to retreat from the sun and in doing so, finding a location optimal for looking at pics that may or may not have happened last night. Quirky, Logan hoped for a few of the photos to be a deviant construction of dreams. In most cases this was actually true, leading to the feeling of a habit that led to greater enjoyment for the participants rather than those hoping to showcase in a traditional gallery setting. Strange to know a wall was more difficult to please compared to the lucky constraints that hung around a loose evening spent on one's craft.

Logan exclaimed a few more times followed by grunts closely related to older people expanding from recliners, found two feet attached to shoes still willing to work. Slight pain did follow but nothing severe enough to cause more concern. Just the same, it's a miracle all the parts still had a location not worth abandoning. Expressly, the joints married to arms always agitated by the overuse of the circle rotation that is required to make a U-turn.

None of this really mattered as long as the finger that took the photos still wanted to be on the team. In a lot of ways, the rest of the body was just along for the ride. It's a wonder there was never a coup on the pointer finger from the rest of the enslaved bones stuck doing its will for minimal nutrients. In the end the brain must really have favorites, otherwise all parts would be used equally. That is, if the body is a temple and not just some electric car mass-produced to meet a current revenue stream.

All ballets aside, there is a great appreciation for everything pulling together in partnership to work one more day. Let's face it, some creatives are lucky to make it this far and if they do well, their very journey is now sold to those stuck in long-term degrees. Deep breath. That will just have to wait to be divulged in another story.

Alive, Logan found solace in the ability to stand corrected. It was nice, related to a feeling that provoked encouragement. Far from home in mind but so close to reasoning drenched in familiarity. Cause was not a wonder if not a symptom of understanding of factors that made reality comfortable. Waning from those very withdrawals the three block walk home was simple but daunting. This short trail might as well have been a pilgrimage brought upon by the sun otherwise known as midday. In any tune, the alternative of being labeled homeless was not attractive.

Key, door, floor and eventually bed was the only viable solution upon return. It would not be until darkness that Logan could form the treasured ability to resurface as a human still dealing with Earthly matters. At any rate, the sun had intention to kill while the moon only offered those lonely at night a feeling of camaraderie. Don't hold this moment to truth, just take a walk then reply with your findings. As did Logan, stuck with pressure in the night, while on the other hand at risk of this entire insanity ending poorly.

Luckily, the images have turned out fair enough so far to pass as small rectangles of royalty. Light, sound and even balance fared to meet standards of any court. In reality who cares? That said, judging was also a lively jurisdiction living well in multiple professions loading to green double standards being alive and well. In other words, even insane people still pushed their nonsensical beliefs onto creation in guise to persuade the inspired to forge in their image. Religion, Hitler or Oprah will not be the last ones to do so. Don't even bring in the few ruling families enjoying technology capable of controlling the weather. Again, another ranch for another time. Between us, the found freedom must still be fighting the half life because uncontrolled banter is keeping its heat.

Aside from the water slide of photos there is this, trash cans versus couch pillows. In the last selection of a time better spent in the end, arose the visual imagery of one good pillow that belongs to a set stuffed diagonally into a square receptacle. Now, this was just not any ordinary pillow with a magical pattern. Huh, the couch cushion had its own way about it. Why would someone toss out one pillow from a sofa in a diamond fashion that left the otherwise compatible shape exposed on top of a square. We are only left with the explanation that supports those who tossed the item out, who still felt that this question had a value.

An afterlife, from whatever was going on in this moment. Softness willing to transcend time in effort to recreate itself as the next generation of reborn support humanity has always needed but never had enough technology to pursue. In clarity, the fluff was red while the can green and the date two days after the pick up. Meaning that this was ascendant related or an afterthought. Leaving the driver in a passing car to ponder what human or pet had failed unexpectedly causing the sudden need to particularly read the hobbled object as belonging to a set of objects still enjoying the comfort of function.

Another wave as this one comes only to be met by a similar relative. Again, again, again, stories translate from imperative into vocal while leaving names in the acquaintance category. Pulse of persuasion takes a fair time to eat away at normal behavior. Logan, beneficial to have made it from ground floor finds imperative lessons in tossing hours around in the fashion of a pet toy. Only difference in this moment is the pet or toy.

Logan, confused even with himself on what that could mean rolls over to introduce the left shoulder with his face, flooring itself happily to feel the grounding below. This day is to be spent on nothing but leaning into a unique fashion in hopes to change the light on this subject.

Chapter Eight

After Day

Only in passing can the clarity of understanding another day position itself to care with little ideals to comfort, surrounding undertakings needing compensation. Otherwise known as not knowing about a darn thing but still stuck in the fact that something that you do must be delivered by a particular date. That in itself is a really unfortunate human concept, let alone the knowledge that we are people trying to figure out patterns.

Parking that overload destined to be a rant, need overtakes first, hammering, while we all bend in the middle to prove our younger selves have a body. Aside, museums want what they need to make cash flow leaving the sneaker pirates to seek treasure. Another night falls forward, while compassion for the prior one wanes calmly into oblivion.

Logan takes the following two days to eat lettuce while fixating on smoothies. Both inspired by a tortoise or a turtle that once existed in proximity to a garden started for Hayden to prove not all humans hated Earth. Now look, he won't even spill a sneeze let alone a hello. Amber's understandable but talkative nature towards Hayden made for violence and abuse. Stuck with progressive ideals, this alone time did better to bottle excitement found with a closing of a screen.

Morning robbed the side of normality. Clear headed, tremors ran rampant. One twitch, two twitch, three twitch, four twitch. Logan could no longer think about a movement without jerking a body part to fit. Flickering to every notion was harsh but brought into death while sleep removed the curtain. Ignorable, even the Notre Dame burns down, so will poets.

Logan charges the battery in a one lens camera. Reparation is everything if it's not lost heritage willing to be later sponsored. Face the facade, cash is the only way modern times will fix historic snails looking for a bigger home. Why not set fire to the underfunded to get those willing to provide opportunity to hand over what little wealth is reserved. Smaller pockets retrieve large gains as long as the dogs on foot only know I'm the one running away. Heading hand in hand still dealing with a prospect, this head fell on a sharp prospectus, left in a library closed to human visitors in particular for thier general safety.

Thank goodness books over food is not a concern and idealisms inhabits structural decomposition, leading our power devices to turn cold. Breathing, there will only be a few needed nights like this. Tuned, ready and prepped, the next family awaits from the purple preparedness.

Meaning that you are ready while everyone around has a great sense of misunderstanding. Easy when the factor of communication takes majority role with short videos that were purposed to explain youth while teaching sexual behavior. Even if what was expressed was not intentional, we will all look backwards and feel such. After all, a welcome is no greater than a hello if the wording is fitting to those able to understand. That's why teaching is powerful and a secret manor.

Logan stretches to forget while breeding Friday. Another day peaks its head over the clouds while the population on Earth learns to behave around a sphere they are familiar with. Not easy considering the amount of others in the general way to happiness. Regardless, each day is a gift to Logan and that means more to him than the overwhelming desire needing to fulfill a lazy standard. No, life is definitely a poppy field of expression deserving to be harvested for the flowers before others can misuse the nature of the beast. Once corrupted there's no saying what might happen to the farmer or market willing to harvest the crop with multiple satisfactions. It's probably best to just act like the rain and ignore the journey to focus on returning while brushing off what is left behind.

Jovial, Logan finishes another morning smoothie thinking about what it would feel like to have a conversation with weather. Are the conditions emotional or natural? Is there really a seasonal pattern or are we guessing about what is to come? Logan sits back, turns on the daydreams and contemplates if *The Weather Channel* employees have a happier marriage than the rest of the non-scientists. Not that it matters but truly knowing when a storm is possible could be power. That said, never let a meteorologist talk to your spouse.

With all this potential excitement to explore the day came the meander. Out the window, as if a lazy dog spotted a slow line frisbee. Joining the month were shadows of a promising dark evening that very well could lead to an even more covert night. The kind perfect for capturing unrelated loathing in the halls in front of his garden neighbors. Being a weekend, it did mean there was risk. Drunks might be misusing their transportation but on the other hand that would be an added thrill. Human versus normal behavior sounded a little weak but the sequel had promise. Decided, all that was left was the hope he had remembered to plug in the camera. Without power the night would be silent and beers poured over long lines of drivel on the subject of what might have been.

Inspection proved worthy of another escape from the constant known as home. All there was left to do is collect outside attire, willing to match the current circumstance. In this case, jeans, factory boots, jean shirt and the ambition to handle what might linger in undesirable locations found in front of everyone's dwelling.

Oddly enough, we park our cars in garages behind the home, while leaving trash in front blocking the view of the flowers. Meaning, we care more about our ability to get to work then our appearance. Now that we all work from home, look at all the cars that live on the street or are simply left in the driveway. If there ever was proof we no longer care about much as a society, this is it. We have finally concluded that it is okay to show our trash alongside our car and front entry because in reality none of it belongs to us anyway. It's the same concept as why we used to let our children play in the streets. Only this time kids have no rights and are consumed by the notion that their future might be a tiny home located in their parent's backyard. Truthfully, it's a shed but there's no reason to be mean.

At least they will be located away from the trash, behind the car and tucked safely away with the shovels. It's simply wild how crazy life can become when there are a few years of existence that resemble the shape marbles and bubbles trying to represent us with valid attampts towards matching completion.

One, two, three, Logan refocused on the air entering busy lungs in strain to collect then release a fickle atmosphere hovering around this moment. By bending the paper clip from the desk into every possible shape then pieces, he could tell his mind needed to be distracted in spades to remain clear-headed as when this project started.

In multiple complicated ways it was hard to quiet the hand let alone the lines it felt obligated to micro-manage. A sick carnage of memories tried to help while hiding behind an alternate goal set to poke holes in the days after it's to participate. This moment and others like it were the gate before relapsing into a world full of short days and gifts by sleep. Noticing is triggered. Logan quickly stood up to stretch out a clean shirt that hung to a frame that had grown thick from coldness while the cloth shrunk from heat.

Regardless of who was to blame, the newly found sickness was confused about understanding the past that needed to be shrugged off. Furthermore, there were collections of people all over the world waiting for what might be Logan's best work yet. If not in the reviews, most certainly in the eyes of those spending nights passed out on sidewalks around town. Laughing to himself still about the night before, precautions sparked only to be evicted by a careless center between a soul and brown boots.

Bang! The coffee pot cooked its own hole in the depression and just like that our sun found its way through the blinds. After a few sips everything seemed to be okay just as fast as it was conjugated. Yes, the day would be left with hazy ways, besides preparation for another night exploring the micro caves of rubbish left representing coal mines once belonging to hard-working families displaced by bad luck, dying Earth, or laziness married with overwhelming health issues willing to pull the trigger on multiple generations of workers at once.

With all of that said, you're reading the end of another month holding hands with trash day. The exploration should be fresh if not completely virgin for such travelers. This was also true due to the previous ongoing pandemic, killing off any fun related to touching a stranger let alone their personal belongings. For some reason that didn't worry Logan, as a floating particle engrained the idealism that he was immune to such weird explanations for why people disappeared out of the living.

Such desires left a prime opportunity for those willing to roll the dice on their health. Going off of Logan's previous habits not to mention the current ones this was not even a spot of concern. As long as the project found some light while his eyes remained open finishing was the only objective. After all, at the end of the day it's hard to say what will be left when we're taking aim in person and body.

Again, Logan drinks some more coffee but this time with whiskey as a chaser as the sun has just now retired to greet others in more healthy location of the planet. Regardless, the packing for tonight's outing must begin. With a simple black backpack Logan planted photo capable machines, a blanket for another night on the sidewalk, a canteen filled with wine, two rags for sticky situations and cleaning the moisture off multiple lenses, one notebook hardly used, two pens and a photo of Amber with Hayden for good luck.

There was something almost ceremonial about packing for a voyage holding unique dangers that most people at home would never face in a lifetime let alone multiple times before, during, then after an art show. It could be the pressure of being great but realistic danger lives in habits unwilling to die beside a person not willing to try for a better legacy. Even if those vices did not have the body's best interests in mind, tonight was decided back when Logan ate overdue lunch.

With a cracking of the back door, Logan found the night air had once again partnered with the heat produced by blacktop getting to know tropic wind patterns. In so many ways this was the perfect night if only there was a cool wind produced in an occasional cloud willing to black heaven's lights. Besides that, the buzz was perfect in the amount to mount day two of *Trashed*.

As relatable to many nights, this one also had the promise of cats, sleepless dogs abandoned outside with the occasional insomniac doing what they can to express how normal it was for us to be on the streets at 1:00 a.m. In their defense, most of the time their handheld leach was attached to an excuse that was also worried about being judged while keeping its distance too.

With only a few more steps needed to lead the way to towards the Mackenzie home, feeling positive was easy. Especially due to the imagery of what looks like a home turned on its side then dumped out. Stuff bleeding from the front door past the mailbox onto the curb found freedoms when the breeze down the road carried what was light enough to dream about into distant yards.

Everything went everywhere doing what little stuff could do in preparation for the staged dumpster flirting with an overly aggressive looking bulldozer. If there would be an end to Earth this picture captured how hard disregarded nuances wanted to jail break into space with no regrets about the damage done to its current occupancy.

By how the debris didn't apologize towards landscaping, it was clear the present owners had died with no kinfolk left to stop the invasion. Paper swarmed around mocking waste dating plastic bags fleeing into the area enjoying weightlessness from humanity. Broken chairs sulk, furniture wept, headboards more than footboards gave in towards circumstance. Plastic cracked, cloth soaked up the nightmare with heavy eyes, gravity held down shoes, plates, suitcases, electronic boxes, kitchen tables all while books greeted grass well, molding eternally in killing the planet externally. Boxes tried to mimic tombs but lacked dexterity. Another explanation would be careless cardboard that couldn't care less about structural demands. Even those vintage boxes left over from the original move tired of holding belongings that they could not relate to. Aside from futility, there were the guilty. Broken fans, light fixtures, cracked yard statues, shattered glass in frames and the most important, old developed pictures.

Someone's life started here after finishing somewhere else then became what is known to as an end. Probably, an unforeseen conclusion but one regardless of the idealism feeding reason. Years had been a steppingstone in a wandering dream until the factory slowly turned inward. Now, their trash circulates freely, then their remnants helped guide the decision for expansion. In modern times what was really important is buried beneath society's contributions to their life which lays in ruins with its own freedom to pollute willingly amongst those left. The most brilliant trash will find its way into a better maintained yard, while others simply are blown lost down the city sewers.

Set, Logan's tripod opens in a place for perceived action. Still a block away, the tragedy of this site is felt from countless yards due to the unexplainable mail found miles away. Excitement is afoot, even more so when the reality of no trash cans becomes clear.

If the owners did not even bother to use a trash can, they most likely did not go through the trash they were throwing out. A solid sign of what was to come and effort to produce what might be Logan began the process of naturally capturing the moment from first glance.

In the premier few captures, moments are broadly covered in a wide span of understanding. With a larger shot of what is to be homed in upon it is easier to understand what may follow. If you're on the outside, then you're looking in has the ability to create a world belonging to only itself in the mirror. Leaving each soft step of perspective with new advancement towards the hardest moment we all reach.

Understanding our selected treasures in this snapshot actually will be collected measures on another's time. Yes, this child is a representation of what they, we, I, and you are but in retrospect, that's it. Things might need left out but words with unique tones will always be lost to an ear spacing a sentence of being deaf.

Logan hung his head to focus on other aspects. The shoes that carry the body full of creative drive, hoped for utopia as explained by Joan the novelist, tonight with all of its purpose and most importantly enough freedom still around the core of being able to dig through other people's trash without getting in trouble. Laughing, that is probably the best attribute about this neighborhood.

Head back up, the next home came to focus. A one-story, three small bedroom home with one bathroom. Day-to-day operations went well for over seven years but now represented nothing more than a hideout from hangovers. Young, well off, with idealism on the flat Earth theory made for one epic journey unable to sustain loyalty.

Both participants came to a sober conclusion one night regarding his unwillingness to believe our planet was indeed flat. So, she went off to Colorado while he went back to college. Leaving nothing more than memories of the beach life alongside partial recollections of people who always had too much fun escaping doors at parties.

All of that to the left, it also looked like they took everything with them besides the remainder of the fridge locked in one plastic bag and sealed by the curb. Oddly enough, it's never the worldly interesting people that leave out sophisticated, interesting trash.

It's actually the older folks not willing to show any signs of interest that end up being the best storytellers, uncovered and waiting to be stumbled upon by examination. This is in part just for the fact that most young people have not been around long enough or adequately patient for anything truly inspiring to happen. Along those lines, previous generations had more opportunity for wealth accumulation if not in numbers than most certainly in practice. Gaining and living as a whole sum can equal in amount to prosperity if taught correctly. Pursuit to follow practice seems to be the key.

Shaking his head, Logan felt too caught up in this undeliverable to continue for their energy towards the other plastic bag of perishables. No worries, there were a few more homes on the list tonight still promising a gateway into culture long-forgotten currently practiced by those coming then going. In every bit of art, the beginning is a search, middle profound and by the end drowning in the attempts to not ruin the middle.

Feeling short-handed, the space between discovery and arrival still compared to the years that must have been left in between collecting a life dialogue. Without reason, orphaned alone, great respect must be given towards the ruins left in this pattern. Not stylized this particular act of removal operated in the same effort as a purge. Better known and described as a spring cleaning. Let it go, came simply, forgetting to understand the nuance of matters without divulging them into comfortable centuries. What better way to say goodbye to the ones you love than to start complete annihilation of every item still holding on to what memories were created by that crap.

Revealed, Logan could feel the pressure of being overly observing, leaving the very situation subject to rancid philosophy. Overthinking had become new to this moment. Just in time to assist clarity, being free is exactly what is needed for a photo shoot such as this one.

Click, click, an electric camera mocks the sounds of the past. With that particular sound still welcome to each photo as it falls off the edge of space and time with the evening. Paper blowing off a desk left victim to the wind seems to have the same effect. Only in this case, there's no telling what is on the papers while instead the pictures seem to easily communicate.

From the looks of all this, Logan is alone in his fascination towards an outcome that used to understand the lifestyle of those living here. Snapshots linger longer while this experiment is focused on how we can communicate in a way that will abruptly end.

It's questionable if either has the ability to last further than the other. Feeling the line, Logan continues deeper into the perceived situation. Boxes, upon boxes of antiquated tape stick out presenting a sore thumb. Half a dozen dresses and six men's shirts also stand their ground in blocking access to deep collections. In many ways, whoever tossed this stuff out felt layers with her best friend. In doing such, levels of more complicated strata of paper came to light.

At this second, digging had begun. What was hidden? Who buried these things and did they really hide them all or were they just too distraught to understand what was going on? Everyone knew, as most of the time they do. It's a fantasy to try and reconstruct hope from the debris. Even if all you find are examples of love once rendered, there is a loss of the very same. At that notion Logan took a moment to reconsider his trespass before moving forward with a goal.

Locate the story, express what was once daily life and if at all possible, over-exaggerate what happened in order to prove shallow holes have great leaders circling back to being humble.

Counting each breath, Logan went forward with the exhibition outline. Capturing everything from dresses, ties, underwear, holiday cards, then the unthinkable. Personal journals, diaries, medical scripts, lists, ending in ceramics made by youth.

It seemed that the escape was vigilant if not forced, in the matter of life spacing death. Whoever left here no longer needed their personal belongings, let alone a sense of being in society. Unlike the past or present it is not worth bringing enough literature to create such. So here we are, Logan on the road taking pictures of what all of our ultimate outcomes end up being.

Pressure aside, it feels good to know we don't have to clean up after ourselves. Positioning the kitchen cabinets next to the old sink, a red medicine box drops towards revival. Close towards Q-tips, this box was set clean as it had been used in recent months. Simply marked with a sterile representation of the medical cross the idea of being interesting came fast and slow out of some precaution of what occurred there in the last hole. Still, the red box that belonged to an elder was too much fun in the light of finishing what was left of Logan's preparations.

Swaggering around, keeping sea level was balanced amongst manners that tried to respect an upright mobility. Enough quarters paid, Logan picked up the last item. The intention to return it to the curb came first but it was settled with a color much closer instead.

Pops down the vault seemed more unpredictable then previously observed. Leaving multiple moments going towards not understanding childproof containers. Crack, red opened with a sense of relief. Too unworried about the labels, Logan cracked a few more round containers over dodging whatever may come as the effects settled in.

The camera was packed along with anything important. Whatever just happened was going on fast enough to blur any outcome that would be. The curve itself became cooler as the caller transformed into Jell-O. Not trying to be mean but thankfully whoever lived here was dead because Logan or at least his body was soon to follow their path physically.

Slam, on his back and set near an electrical wire owned by a crow laid twenty feet in front of what was left of vision. A partner bird quickly joined the first one while making sweet comments in a hooting fashion. For a while they sat in love, trading comment about rats and other easy to catch vermin that ran around on the ground. Oh, did they mock those of us who could not fly or begin to understand what it meant to comprehend possibilities related to gliding. This was their language far from my own but completely relatable when it comes to flight romance. As the old man said, we all dream of, *The Danger*, or so follow freedom in the form of feathered communication.

A low hum relaxes what was otherwise known as focus, leaving a sense that we all are just waiting to be extracted from one form or the other related to waste. A plastic duck falls out onto the street forming one of Logan's disturbances. Landing upright, on the road a few fifteen feet away after the wind held it fast. Upright, each car runs it over. Squeak, squeak, squeak and so on having no identity towards the photographer left stranded in the art that was selfish to begin with.

Clasping forward in a backwards yard, a moment that represented eating dinner, breakfast, lunch ending in dinner before Logan realized his current situation was separate from its aspirations. This sun must be lazy in comparison to the last. If not in brightness, then in haziness. Joking aside, the packed blanket came to no use, so did the unworkable notebook. Left with the task of killing oneself had newly transformed grass into moisture that once again struck Logan into focusing on if anyone had noticed him.

Alone, still in this compromising position, relief brought sadness in the form of not being noticed. Lifting from a solid constraint, ability refocuses from eternity into existence willing to overcome prospects of altered metamorphosis. Otherwise known as another world full of opportunities lingering on a dreamcatcher left with little wind now cursing windchimes to break all the peace. Bird baths are left too wet today, in concert to work with containers of bird seed supplying pallets looking for revenge on territory otherwise left parched.

Drifting from here is easy until it's not perceived as a total of thirty waste of objects. Another sunrise was greeted by a human yard ornament, too old to not recognize the signs of a rising sun on Earth, even if the temple that housed a circular saw of a mind was decrepit, in a New York City alleyway and definitely not likely to be enhanced by scarred ruins of the ancients.

No, Logan O'Lakes was wet, smelly, surrounded by trash and appeared mugged. After understanding this, his eyes still worked but arms were attached to stiff twigs, moving in flaps around searching for the camera, still willing to have an attachment towards his crap.

Out of relief, old technology still remained engaged in the journey. Happy about this, there was also a feeling of dread, knowing very well that he would never throw the camera away but as long as he held it prisoner to a battery, he would find more mornings like this one.

In many ways, this device was intended to capture the moments that also provided excuses to squander yawns. Addiction is known to enjoy the company of creative people, especially those willing to make big risks towards the arts and finding help.

Still watching the sun chase the night sky that was turning orange in declaration to mark victory in battle. Even if winning meant losing after only a few hours. Another day was offered to one more dawn that would be chased. This time, it hopefully was going to be a clean night but that's just the game when it comes to exploring others' leftovers. More so if those people are strangers and you never had the opportunity to examine the condition of the refrigerator let alone make or model. Metal scrappers usually get to appliances pretty fast, making judgment on food preparation and hygiene being difficult. On the flip side, these aren't just some pitted plates needing tossed out from living comfortably retired in a kitchen cabinet that was too high up to reach. Makes one wonder, what is left out of reach and forgotten in ourselves.

Sniff, sniff, sniff, sniff, Logan prematurely heard the sound of sniffing around the circumference of his head. Looking towards the east hoping it wasn't a rough pygmy pig, the center of his eye met with a small pink tongue with a black dot on it.

Wet, the listening continued until he was blinded in one eye and sitting up in the distress that only confusion could deliver. Wiping out the animal who kisses an elderly woman came to focus. Four gracious feet, tall, wearing a yellow dress over black tights tied together with blue sneakers and a sweater.

"Honey, oh honey, are you okay?" Charged in a whisper, a figure asked with concern.

Still stunned mixed with no ability to focus through such intense morning sun, Logan did what any sane human would do, raising both hands out to his side in the fashion of wings he yelled, "Haw, haw, haw, haw, haw!" While flapping uncontrollable arms around and attempt to fly.

Abruptly stopping, just as fast as was started, then shot the intruder the whites of his eyes.

Both creatures on either side of the leash just looked onward with the words of judgment, "Well then Birdman, you're obviously busy." Speaking beast pulled on the smaller one, repeating the line, "Come on Snowball, this ostrich does not need our help."

Finishing quickly, a car ran over the duck as it was being too late to be parked at a job site. Squeak! Connecting to the sound alone, Logan was tossed back towards sobriety. Quickly realizing his mistake from the night before, all understanding of why the older person could not help instead of flying away which caused further suspicion towards reality.

Logan was not a bird, but in fact a photographer that occasionally took pictures of them. Gathering what clarity was making itself available was the next subject of focus. This was going to be harder than what might be expected through the lens of the encore. Yes, Logan was dressed properly for a day like this one and yes, he did meet the requirements of looking human. What was still going on inside made the mile walk back to the studio

unreachable, full of its possible sinkholes posing as
potholes of promise to be fixed by the city. Only when a
person like Logan was sacrificed into one of these holes
would change actually happen.

Then there's all the joggers, morning walkers,
mixed with people simply looking for a conversation from
any stranger willing to entertain them but honestly
bragging about Monday and accomplishments like
children. All of that is enough to cause anxiety but the very
real possibility that they may also turn into abstract
paintings flat-out haunted any notion of walking home.

After a few more attempts to fly, the squeak of the
plastic duck on the road congealed with hundreds of close
up pictures of the trash he had become. Dinnertime had
well packed on with high chances along with visual
alterations of the environment he might encounter outside
of his current yard. Ready to stand, one foot talked to the
other knee and wouldn't you know, movement went
forward in a smooth progression of positive mantras, while
all along avoiding eye contact with mailboxes in order to
dodge the shame they'd like to give after someone had a
long unexpected night out on the town. Don't even ask

what trash cans would cast rumors about, luckily it wasn't their workday.

For Logan to travel one mile in a safe defeat it would take around three hours if you count the time he stopped to address censored garage lights ending their shifts for the evening. One diversion did offer a cup of coffee from a thermos out of concern but in reality, who knows where that thermos has been? Besides, there was no time to stop for a chat. If Logan was going to make it back home to sleep with the next day then return to the streets with any sense of scheduled focus it had to be applied towards this series of work. Besides, trash day was rapidly approaching, leaving fun escapes miles apart from forgetful homeowners who do to not realize what day it had been.

Click, thump, click went the back door lock. Looking over his shoulder Logan address two silent friends sitting full of plastic bags floating in water, "Hey you two, I'm back but not for long. Did I miss anything?" Silence brought guilt, so he emptied the water from both Amber and Hayden before returning inside for a ham sandwich. After that, batteries were returned to their homes but the entire house went into a deep moment of rest.

Not one or two or three days but a week went by before consciousness returned in a waking body to the living cause. Aware at first, then not caring second, Logan felt thirsty. Accumulating every beer in the fridge, spoiled wine went second with little delivery of impact. Confused by the lack of inspiration the only reasonable solution was to check the mail.

Click, click, click the front door was moved upon its hinges. Oh, there was the mail. Three boxes of wine, crowned by letters from far-off galleries wishing to schedule a time to view his latest series. All of it was intoxicating. It's just, some of it would be more fun than others. More so the items in the boxes that were actually containers and did not pretend to be letters. Brushing off the top dust into the bushes, Logan brought his breakfast inside. Out of all the modern-day miracles, home delivery of wine leveled with the light bulb.

Only difference was one could still work by candlelight and for that matter moonlight or the simple reflection of a glow stick. Players will not last long enough with dynamite but just might be the outcome desired. So now in this day and age we are lucky to have it all.

Daydreaming, love secretly cannot wait for his conversation with delivery drones. In any event the air felt perfect for wandering around flat roads in search for stacked treasure full of unique surprises increased after such a rest that brought dreams focused on a spaceship named *The Goose*.

Packed, the very door of his home firmly shut with brass latches, Logan stepped out back to say goodnight to his trash cans before walking down the driveway and taking a left hand turn. At moments like this he wished for a dog smart enough to understand direction so he could say 'left,' or 'right,' and a companion would follow. If only it wasn't for other parts of this experiment a dog would have been perfect. Resting easy on the correct human choice there was only trash where dictating should be in this moment of the path.

Tonight in particular helped with the promise of three homes worth of material. First, the pullers. A few days prior, the Dad caught Mom cutting up credit cards that he was not aware of. Not so bad until the fact that she had not paid them off first. Just like money likes to do it broke up the entire family. Mom and Dad work everything out but that's only after the fight of a lifetime left ten years of happiness traded curbside. Fresh material mixed with overreacting always displayed well.

Calling people have order while those already confused don't have time for such recollection. We are talking about underwear on top of busted TVs mixed with clay art made by their kid's dramatic cell. No one and nothing was able to escape this type of carnage.

Now, located directly in front of the pile of yesteryears, Logan felt energy of every direction throbbing off the piles of unbagged home goods. How two grown adults can feel so comfortable about leaving so many pairs of socks everywhere astonished even Logan. Amber would have really got a kick out of this location.

Pink socks, socks with frogs, black socks, short socks, socks with holes, new packs of socks, green socks and even some laced ones. All scattered throughout the yard in way that the occasional viewer might wonder if this was some sort of new modern garden technique.

On the other hand, they did add a splash of color that went really well with the white new home in the background. More so the confusion of foot coverings camouflaged other madness no longer visible enough for neighbors quick to be concerned. Such things like wedding pictures, a pogo stick, cracked kitchen trash cans with a box of unused bags.

Making camp, Logan went to work with the idea behind this photo shoot that was to treat the socks like flowers. Shooting each piece of cloth and design for there to be a resemblance of a rose blooming, a potted plant dying, daffodils wilting then tossed aside. His favorite was the bicycle with its basket full of neon foot souses beautiful and just returning from a local market with a barrage of hand picked love for their home. Still rolled up in a ball fresh from the drive in a nearby field.

Following a few hundred shots of the garden by Logan focus went out on a limb to find those parts that lay unmatched, while hanging softly over everyday items society would never associate with socks. Blenders full of singles sitting next to a mini fridge withdrawing from toe coverings. Still, chasing yards is better experienced this level-headed. It's hard to say what would happen if this sample was last. After the discovery of the street drain now clogged from the washed away shoe partners, Logan began feeling a little worried about the moment a small medicine cabinet confirmed they took what was needed as it was empty but he was okay with that, as the photos turned out perfect and needed little editing.

Walking on words while enjoying a donated coffee cup of well branded fully marketed wine, it was moments like this Logan wondered how other influencers felt about being tagged like cattle and he came to gifts received in the mail. But should someone really buy a product just because it was the one abused in a photoshoot, in some stranger's yard in front of an empty home? Honestly, Logan was waiting for the day. Who cares what products found a way onto a t-shirt without a registration mark?

Luckily the walk between abode number one and two was only a few blocks, otherwise this man might have eventually found marriage. As an approaching ship to the extremities of the situation, evidence showed small. That is until complete arrival. Instead of stacking their trash upwards, this particular vagabond lays their goodbyes flat. That's right, every item was tossed out then laid horizontal to the ground. Commitment items like dressers, tables, chairs all mutated in accord to not take any space higher than the knee. If there was a chair, next to it was four detached legs. A dresser looked deflated and so did the drawers not to mention the pillows free of stuffing left as thin sheets that draped neatly. Items like mattresses were left alone but all upside down with old news applied in the fashion of wallpaper placed laying in the grass only three pages high, while clothing reserved seven levels up in space. In fortune, this home was empty upon the time of Logan's arrival because this entire yard was covered front to back in flat display.

No socks, oddly, but massive amounts of horrid supplies. Rows upon rows of toilet paper, napkins and water bottles polluted clean cut grass. In many ways it felt familiar but who in their right mind would move out only to display the contents of where they live in such an attack that defiles explanation or any commands to be alive in moments we can't comprehend as before or after survivors. Photos were now leaping into memory as never expected. It's one concept to find well placed blue chairs neatly stacked with precision but this level of dedication to trash disposal is historic. Further digging found even more well-placed layers.

It seemed the closer to the ground the item the more important it was to this person's survival mentally. It hit Logan O'Lakes like a brick. If she stacks her items out in an order of importance, where are the items of most value? On the bottom like this scenario or just the opposite, on top?

A quick note landed in crude four-letter communication scratched for Amber and Hayden. No longer distracted by paper, the camera clicks sparsely, this time focusing on the items completely flat with the ground. From this lower perspective it was clear to see that Logan had occupied the front yard previously in a game, never willing to share their story out of guilt but also from loving anything worthwhile as long as it felt right. So, from the lowest collection it was clear to see how relationships of one gender identity had settled for reflections.

Regardless, it wasn't the beginning that mattered as much as it was abandoned when the journey had started. Ground-level if you will, on a life that only needs the knees to understand where it's going to an eventual landing, ultimately to find that descent as the means to announce that we have arrived on an entirely new planet with its own rules. Click, the sound reminds Logan of locking the front and back door. That was also the last show of the night before the discovery of box #7. Sitting forced onto the ground to match the height of the other important items all pressed on trying to fight for ground zero.

Deep inside laid the ender. Distilleries holding out in a cave waiting on another terrorist attack from uneasy overthinkers. Bottles collected but not observed, Logan spent another few hours subjectively close to being down to Earth. For the first time in a short breath the sun meets the yard not occupied by a photographer trying to capture its understanding of beauty.

In fact, that day the giant ball fed grass. It was a little lonely but no one understood as to why was Logan made it home safely. He had nothing to do with the day, only focusing on the night. Leaving the sun's reach ineffective to the well-being of this particular creative. Truthfully, about by the time the celestial giant throws the dance away to night, Logan was home in bed sleeping off dreams born from his own body chemistry. Terrifying but still natural when it came to dealing with being alive. For that, this rest only lasts the same amount of time an average person comes to expect.

Shuffling alive only a day later, Logan was levelled when it came to the small amount of time he had been out. Being would go a lot slower if he kept up with this type of behavior. Laughing towards this recollection that he was alive, it still hurt in a way that understood slow music while misinterpreting cellos.

Logan tossed two feet towards the bedroom floor. One warm foot felt the cold tile wild the cold foot felt, well nothing. Waiting a minute for both to collaborate towards walking there's a time to see what it meant for a crowd's willingness to understanding togetherness. Weak, even now, the calling was a foolish one in the eyes of those with any sense of direction. Logan was lucky when passion had proposed meaning, other than dropping from bridges in effort to undermine authority could be seen as a hobby. Still, being titled a free jumper gives a purpose when it comes to carelessness.

Bing, bing, bing, Logan's automatic coffee pot goes off. Like always, Joe goes off way before the receiver is ready. Doesn't matter much, as the conversation is rich with a full body, even though an upgrade is much needed from drip to press. Difference between one is far faster than the counterpart. Joking aside, both require ample sugar and cream.

Cup in hand with little spacing between what has happened between now and no, there's a full day of being alive away from the project willing to be explored. How much detail or why is not really known but being free from the task that defines one's life is always pleasure. Not to mention a day off from direction, from self or boss can never be bad unless that freedom leads to heinous acts that are not self-expression. Laughing out of the emotion of those still facing tiny roles in a screenplay well-suited for larger amounts of fame, sounds of flipping help cure any heartache. If this be a day off than let those be. Sugar from a glass jar melts with already creamed caffeine.

Further stories are fed by the airways that attempt parallels towards relating suffering and truth behind the curse following fame. Attempting when you can get away is worth robbery when talent owns the getaway car. Just ask everyone who has never been caught then pardoned by a president. Knowing freedom starts with understanding who we are talking towards? In this scenario, all of those wanting a reform other than liquidating its masses knows poverty. Even if the majority of us, the people, belong in such a state because we are lazy. Hanging his head, Logan shakes the thought of anyone being such. Correcting a tired mind's hopes for survival insinuates a doctrine. Of course, it's been around for a moment but needs relayed once in a while. Walls disagree with the minority.

It was not often Logan found himself home when raising out of a dream. Or by playing to far off lands to exploit the unknown shielded from the West. In many ways, this type of absence from the start position was preferred. Home in more ways than one, with silent boredom. Never into staying seated for too long, most modern pleasures held glittering entertainment. It was not so much content but the delivery that made devotion to such things difficult to digest.

Why look at a mountain featuring pretty people if you could go there physically and rendezvous with the weather? That's all relationships are in essence, the very reasoning behind a great photo. If someone sees a picture of a field of flowers but can't also comprehend in their imagination what that place smells like an emotion is lost with dirty bathwater. That's at least how Logan felt about his own work.

Very slow to grasp, a photograph had to deliver a sense of immersive environment by pulling out memories associated with familiar touch. A photo of the cold snow in the Rockies is especially cold if the viewer has had a long walk there on a lost road, frozen and uncomfortable. Bright sun, seawater tastes like salt or surf for all of those living with an ocean. Pain, because we all fall down once or twice. Trash was all of this combined.

It's not the original handbook. Every item large or small starts with a new association until interacting with the object ultimately kills the item. Stuck with the choice to repurpose or let go we are forever impacted by the thing. So, when those experiencing a moment of passing pass the trash, all of us remember some part of the ritual, rather it's dragging the can or the items to the curb or the very items themselves. Possibly making the practice of taking out the trash one, if not the most common practice connecting all of temerity.

Unfortunately, such conclusions are most likely even more collective than religion. Atheists still produce just as much waste as a priest or equal. Ever loving to wonder, if this connection shared by everyone is actually a copped practice, created by ruling parties in economy to distract us from something.

After all, if we all feel connected in other ways there is little reason to search out a more complicated belief that requires time married to sacrifice. Taking out the garbage now feels as a play on social media when it comes to putting in the work to save ourselves from complete decomposition by those happy to see little, believed from overly busy populations.

Now, thoroughly distracted himself, Logan can't help but wonder about other seemingly less harmful acts he completes without questioning the origin or root purpose of its creation. A little distraught about not truly being individual, that jest in ways held back progression while being advertised as politically correct. Just like the world heading over lands of the native people while trading modern traditions for those long forgotten.

To Logan, this feels like a a plot to prepare the masses for a more tribal future. One where a bunch of people have enough while recognizing a monarch. Possibly more towards feudalism.

Chapter Nine

Living With Home

Starting at home smells like cooked bread, waiting on a bake sale that never happened between those ready to purchase what it feels like to travel a distance, because I was only prepared to pay for a single flight. A sort of banter capable of picking sides, in an angle to misguide or underestimate folks eager to sugarcoat the soft food no longer willing digestion. Same exact way old kitchen cabinets hinge abuse towards unused appliances, keen to trade with any moment that presented a cake. If not so large, then maybe a muffin that felt rich.

Regardless, there is a thing or two to be said about that which relates while holding an arm's length between size, cost and ingredient level. Aside, Logan was actually more of a cookie individual even though his personality did not match any shape of mass production. In perspective, the only reason to form clumps of dessert came from preferred textures in ability to enjoy a supporting liquid of tea, coffee and occasional modern drink of choice.

A nodding head usually was capable of telling people how important it was for a thin frame to avoid most matters of diets. Even if mouthwash mixed with clever occasions could prove innocence towards particulates in the morning. Simple, part of this granulation, a cup of that liquid and success. Needed provisions came to fruition. The containment such as this could go perfectly with a desk finding the day. Truthfully, the desk and the glass would even have the possibility to learn about each other until the moment one went unused then cold in response to words of neglect.

Sitting on a saddle of serenity the drink never had a chance towards the cup, let alone the desk or inhabitants, those occupants who really enjoyed only the heat from the cup and not the contents. A few more vitamins came into focus with their talents. Microwave wanted to heat the bagel and most of a cooked egg while the fridge only wanted to watch as everything abused each other that had once been protected. In some twisted way the refrigerator knew it was only keeping fresh small amounts of time. Parents hold a similar responsibility alongside trees, cockroaches, vultures and those with hands like raccoons.

Logan, still stood alone with the handleless doors of the kitchen cabinets. So many options without handles. If only there was a poor option to add a handle or two then this decision would be easier. At this level of economy and at the rich level hardware on kitchen doors is not an option.

Go searching for utensils only after fingering a smooth door open while marking up the entire situation with previously used fingertips. Meals transform to properly from quick bite into a production, leaving a moth more comfortable to eat seems on a coat rather than understand light and its positive effects in our environment.

Logan paused, losing it now would only prevent the show I'm having, a perspective that included wellbeing for the Earth, while keeping true towards a particular understatement such as deforestation. Well, in food products this happened towards being better suited as the pulp that only a plant or vegetables should produce. Quickly interrupted, longevity aggressively cut through the means of misdirection. Home is beginning to fall to progressively inwards on an already confused mind.

Blocking out the mayhem is possible but only to the point in saying my time is left figuring out the truth. In many cases that truth has been a second look on a wristband. Any haste to understand belonging to this club is actually worth the cost or a ruse for another story, just as willing to chuck the entire ability overboard. With a single toss, relieving the entire motion bares more possibility.

And how much more exactly would be enough to swallow the anxiety guilty of producing what little addiction existed? How much fame labeled as successful is needed to for peace to grow strong enough towards being well-rounded and a positive member of society that rewards those who don't pass out in strange yards for nights at a time? So far, the only accelerant that brought this to light has been the money flow that just never seems to stop in a mind that knows there will always be enough, even if a photo has never been produced for this upcoming show.

People always talk about leaving the past behind while moving forward but what about your savings earned from past actions? Is there not a small part in every dollar that lingers from what has been done? Every exhibition where works were sold now revisits the present time through what financial gain came from the pain. Even if the memory faded, royalties will forever haunt the now.

Logan took a short walk to think this over and find a chair occupied by a table and jug of wine with a dirty cup. Cleaning out the dried remains from last night a fresh glass was poured. This particular chair pointed at a window where the neighbor's trash cans could be seen.

Not recycled, but they did take it upon themselves to feed normal cans to the rim every week. How two people in their fifties could accomplish this was horrific. To the best of Logan's conclusions, they must have only bought products that came in a ridiculous amount of packaging. That or they bought a ton of small items housed in large boxes that acted as a sales gimmick to make the buyer think they were getting a better deal than what the truth was. At any rate if, *Earth's Shipping Yard*, is real, they're definitely going to end up there.

Some time went past with Logan going back and forth with the neighbors. Trash stories and the true purpose of his talent that laid out the situation. In many ways the two socks were connected. One being that there was too much access to whatever was desired, another being a simple lack of control to oversee the situation if the narrative was seeable in true form by the guilty parties. In conclusion Logan went on to finish the jug of wine before tossing the large container into an empty Hayden that resulted in a loud echo followed by, "Ouch!"

"Hey Logan, look out when you're throwing things would you!" In slight disbelief that his old friend who has not said a word in months was now making demands on the style of trash removal procedures, replying, "Uh, sorry about that Hayden, I'll be more careful with the next."

Coughing while lighting up a cigarette, "Do you really think you should drink more tonight?" Amber shot him a disapproving guardian look, then continued, "Don't you have an art show coming up, shouldn't you be focused on that and not your own pity? The people with the gallery are counting on your stupid photos to make them look cool or something."

Still in slight shock, Logan took his seat on the top step by the back door, "Yeah, but it is what it is, at this point. Whatever is delivered they will love or love talking about how bad they are. Either way is a perfectly suitable outcome for photos of trash titled, *Trashed*."

Pausing, Logan inquires, "By the way, where have you two been all this time? It's never been this long of a silence before."

Amber cleared her throat, "Well, going by the procession of bottles you've been tossing into me empty it's probably safe to say inherently you healed yourself. Well, maybe not healed as much as got too high on brain pills and wine so that we were blocked out and quite rudely and abruptly too if we're being honest. Do you know how awful it has been to be stuck with Hayden and his long-winded stories about whatever drives by?"

Finishing her cigarette, "So many times there was an opportunity to just blow over and roll away. Maybe find a cozy, abandoned sewer tunnel, sit around a fire pit and make some nice homeless friends. But no, I knew you would un-fog eventually."

Hayden, sounding nervous with an offended look aimed at Amber, "Well, I stayed through all the packs of cigarettes, just look at how that smoke has stained my right side. I might be annoying but you're damaging. Anyway, the reason for my continual support was, well, was because I'm a square and had no hope of blowing away even if I wanted to."

The three of them sat there for a moment deciding if what had happened between them was enough to cause further trash talk or just move on. Shaking his head, Logan finally spoke, "So we're good?"

"Yeah, there's issues but you're human. You'd never last a few weeks without us," said Hayden as he shot Amber a smirk.

Amber, looked straight at Logan then said, "You really don't know do you?"

"Know what?" asked Logan.

Smashing another drag and tossing it into Hayden she went on, "Well, ever since you found that last prescription, you have been a little way from home mentally, now, spending way too much time at home physically. For starters, you started getting the newspaper every morning in the nude. All of your trash has been taken out but instead of giving it us, you've been disposing of it in the neighbor's can. So much that they had to get a second one."

Stopping, "That actually worked out because apparently Rodger across the street is gay and the second can the city brought over, oh, I think his name is David and he is also gay, they fell in love and have been having the time of their life decorating their small part of the driveway. So, unless you want to be a jerk you might just have to continue to use the neighbor's cans and leave the therapy sessions for us."

Logan, sitting back on his hands while trying to feel how he felt about these actions came to the conclusion there wasn't much energy left to care about all of it, "I see Amber, is there anything else?"

"Besides the fact that it hasn't been just a few weeks, more like a month or so. Logan, those pills really robbed you of your life. You probably should consult the can you pulled them out of. There might be other side effects that inhibit you to drive or live a normal life like you once had." Laughing, Amber lit a third tobacco stick while basking in the panicked look of confusion set in Logan's face.

Logan, "Okay, if it hasn't been a few weeks what date is it then?"

Amber replies, hating feeling worried as well, "A week before your show but just don't ask me the year. I always confuse trash can years with human years. The math is just daunting."

Shaking a little, "A week before? Crap, crap, crap!" filled the air after leaving Logan's mouth as he stood to rush around trying to gather what had been created for the series so far. Only after a moment or two was he actually able to obtain any goals. Then in back, outside with the laptop Logan continue to panic talk. "Okay you two. Oh, I'm going to need your help deciding what photos to you use for the show and what photos might be offensives to disposal containers."

"If you want my help, I'm going to need more smokes and Hayden needs a bath. You'd think a bird might have died in him with that stench." Looking at Amber, Hayden spouted back, "It probably died because it ate one of the cigarette butts that you that you tossed beside me.

"Regardless, that's our demand."

"Seriously? We are finally talking and you feel the authority to make demands?"

"Hey, we had to watch your naked butt get the paper every morning, this is the least you can do for us."

"Fine, fine, I'll get the hose."

"Oh no you don't," said Hayden, "I'm a recycling can, only warm water, Epsom salt and lavender soap will do!" Logan disappeared into the home then returned tossing an old carton he had found at Amber then turned the hose on Hayden. Cold, wet, with the smell of stale paper, the three pushed on.

Harder than expected, the selection process went on slowly to the point every photo took way more time than what should have been required. Amber, Hayden and Logan all have different idealism on what themes the show should encompass. Amber enjoyed the dirtier ones, Hayden was into any shot that had a recycling bin in it and Logan was chasing the use of light that identified with the emotion of what happened to cause the display. Through the fighting, laughing and takes of judgment they selected ten works out of thousands. That might seem small in comparison to availability but the majority of the photos were blurry or of the night sky.

Also in the rejected folder sat seven videos of Logan reciting poetry to various household items. In one particular video, he is telling a rubber duck about undying love only to spend the next hour crying because said duck rolled out of his hand into harm's way where it spent the night being ran over, leaving Logan alone with a disappointed body and the torturous squeak of a plastic bathtub duck. The corresponding journal column titled, 'Plastic Bride,' went something as follows.

Plastic bride, so smooth
Will you shine yellow hue?

If I'm willing & you say I do
How we will float on

In a tub or pond
Oh little duck, will you bring me luck?

But wait, don't roll to the street
Better suitors, you're destined to meet

Come back and quack for me
You are the one that left

So why do you cry when every car goes by?
Are you in pain with my body lame

Or has some danger came?
Our love has gone silent

Please do the same
Your squeaking tortures my brain

The other videos follow this concept but are expressed in numbers instead of letters. Every time Logan reaches a point of lubrication he stops communicating with words and relapses into numbers, depending on the letters and their position in the alphabet. For the majority of the human race, these videos will be concealed until after he dies. Not so much in refrain from tarnishing Logan's pride but so museums will be able to continue to show his madness while profiting from not having to pay.

Regardless, a video of a grown man laying in a yard full of trash reciting numbers of the form of poetry doesn't belong in an exhibition, titled *Trashed*. Or does it? Money is a numbers game and that play has been the deciding factor in the majority of the moves shown in the photographs. There is a strong emotion to video that photos sometimes can't reach. Not to mention it's art so anything is believable if production, not addiction, is the architect. Enamored about this idea for a video, the thought lingered long enough to eventually feel important enough to apply. With the quick addition on the end of a list of works, the final paperwork became signed, sealed then handed off to the carrier pigeon known as email.

Looking up from the laptop, "Well that's it. The email has been sent to my publicist. All that's left is for us to develop our choices."

After a really long pause, Logan repeated himself. Again, after a pause, another representation of the first statement emerged. One more time, a form of the last statement appeared to reach quiet expressions.

Amber and Hayden sat aside as ordinary receptacles instead of friends. No smoking or joking they once again were gone. Happy to have had their help, regardless of the wait, the thought of not drinking more wine over company was no longer a rather pleasant choice. Returning inside with a sense of accomplishment a second jug of wine was open. Instead, this time, by means of being sober, he realized the top did not crack open but simply unscrewed. By the looks of it, a full bottle had already been opened but never drank.

At Logan's home, that was unheard of. At least one glass would have been harvested. Suspicions arose but after the third glass were forgotten. At this point, the lights in the room became too oppressive, leading Logan to question. I've just felt like a collection of shapes, while thoughts of creativity disappeared in the face of easy and usual. Common distractions, like the softness of the kitchen towels, the humor of a silly commercial on the radio all seize the moment off into darkness that was also unaware of the situation.

Even more strange is the lack of desire to drink onwards. Happiness already had been reached in a way that swaggering around could never deliver. Yes, creativity was gone but the baggage with it had also left. Leaving Logan to spend the rest of the night watching reality TV and not feeling one bit of motivation to work on his craft. Let alone, little thought on the pending art show, highlighting instead what it felt like to enjoy popular entertainment, such as the world of streaming.

Re-enlisting Logan, the sun came through the window. The night before it had fallen less severe, while leaving a small trace of evidence to warn about the tainted wine. Finding enough drive to recover distant feet a struggling mind agreed to travel. Oddly, for being a Saturday after a night of prepping for a show, his home looked well put together. The objects were in their places to the point Logan thought it had to have been a cleaning service. Truthfully, the place never looked better, let alone felt this put together. Not one pen or earbud was out of a cup or container. Perfection had arrived.

Well, well, well. Oh, nothing. Oddly enough, none of this felt familiar but more so worried, as for Logan there was also the dreaming aspect. For the first time in his life, Logan did not dream. Not even a little, to the point the majority of it was forgettable. What was going on or better yet, who is controlling this suitable individual, living in a model home, representing upper class middle society?

Sick but not from a hangover, dizziness came back. Only this time he wasn't thirsty but jonesing for something completely different all together. He didn't shake out of being without but from his mind reconnecting with a troubled body.

Quick to respond, Logan headed to the kitchen past the jug of wine, flipped over a cup then drank the tap water like there was a shortage and this was Texas. Filling, drinking, and repeating the last cup felt more comfortable. Attached to a glass of water rather than it being needed as necessity, just like holding a beer at a party but never drinking it. This resulted in landing on the couch with closed eyes, feet up, matching long breaths set open by weighted eyelids.

At first, she looked like an oversized crocheted pillow and that was comforting, until Logan realized he did not own such a pillow. Moments later, the entire figure came into focus with the permission of an over worried mind waking up from atypically clean surroundings. She had to be from the 70s, her hair cut short because of age.

194

The cloth that covered her extremities was all gray besides the gleam of a shark tooth embedded with diamonds that hung around her neck.

With blue eyes, the trail between confused towards controlling felt rather one way in strength. Neither one of us was doing much but observing the other in their natural movements. It wasn't really what this intruder was going to talk about but rather how they would deliver their opening lines. And in all reality, they could take whatever they wanted beside a typewriter on the desk in the end.

Maybe she was a fan? It's hard to really say from the lack of movement emitting signals from her body. In good faith Logan and the elder stopped looking at each other for a long time. Well, a long time for her.

For Logan it was another moment waiting on zoning out, while thinking about the thousand reasons he was in the situation with a stranger not willing to toss the first line of communication out onto the floor. So, more time went by, with the addition of more time followed by more, more, more, more and even more time.

It came to the point eventually that Logan sat up and went about his day. Fiddling with the carrier pigeon emails about the show, eating lunch and eventually taking out trash and prepping dinner. After a glass of wine or two curiosity came in looking like a lost cat. Thinking to himself that there was no way he could go to bed with this lady sitting on his couch, it crumbled.

Walking back over to the living room to arriving at the spot in front of her he asked, "Would you like a cup of tea or something?"

Looking up, the stranger spills out with disappointment, "Well, I was waiting for a hello or good morning, but a cup of green tea will do. Just make it quick, as there is now too much to talk about in the time left over by your stubbornness."

A little tossed by being demanded upon by the trashcans first and now this trespasser, Logan used tap water for the tea in revenge.

"Here you are. Hope you like it."

With sour dressed at the top of her face like a poster stuck on the table, "I think this tastes just like what you have been behaving like around the neighborhood. To make it rather short, I'm here to tell you to stop throwing your trash in our extra can. Please, wear clothing when extracting your paper and finally, most importantly, please take medication on your own, as prescribed on the bottle.

For years now, Logan, I've lived across the way from you, watching everything that goes on. At first it was fascinating but now that I'm retired from the mental health field it's disappointing. I will never be able to relax until you stop being distracting. There are plenty of people we can get you in contact with to start the recovery process."

Taken aback by the attack, Logan replied, "Are you the one that cleans my home?"

Laughing, "Goodness no! But I am the one lacing your wine with appropriate medications for your illness."

"What?!" Questions Logan soberingly, "You're doing what?"

"Logan, look, you're sick and that's okay, you can be fixed. I just don't have the time to look after you anymore. You see, my husband and I are moving to a warmer situation." Taking a clean manilla presentation out of her purse from on the floor, the death nurse from a horror movie handed Logan a folder, "In this, you will find everything needed to keep a healthy mind. All I ask is that you forgive my intrusion and occasional overdose. You know, in all my life I would never have guessed you would drink three jugs of wine so fast. Anyway, how many cups have you had today?"

Feeling woozy, a simple, "Three," left his lips.

"Well, that's great Logan, you'll be out long enough for me to disappear. Just remember, look at the house file when you sober up."

Midway through the next, day Logan reappeared from a cocktail of who knows what mixed with what in the world. Was that person real? Surely enough, a crocheted blanket fell to the floor. Grubby fingers agreed to work in tandem to retrieve Pandora's folder. Flipping it open, a single piece of paper was inside. It was a smiley face printed on cardstock.

That was it, with nothing more than a gallon of perfume still lingering in the room. Inherently being creative, it was not completely out of the question if Logan made the blanket and folder in a fit of lightning late-night debauchery towards his own body. Unlikely but a solid possibility that brought more comfort when thinking about the alternative scenarios.

Landing on the conclusion that if this elder neighbor had been drugging his food in an attempt to change him she could have saved a lot of time by just sneaking around and simply giving him the goods in the trash. Even if abuse was evident, that happened anyway, just through alternative routes.

With all possibilities aside, the incident surprisingly settled quickly with Logan. Most likely, through the understanding that passed over the next few nights, he would forget all about what happened. That and he had a show to prepare for mentally, physically, wardrobe wise and artistically.

None of the photos have been printed, developed or prepared in any fashion or degrees. So far the work would show up in the same fashion as a blind date that already had been on a few dates before this one. Tired, unprepared but interesting enough fulfill the needs of the human body already rendered successfully.

Enjoying the notion that his pictures could go on a date while holding the power of rejection but falling in love too eagerly, made this moment idealist for Logan. Even so, his work was not bent on breaking society from its current behavior but to enlighten the people who could break society of what was really going on in small towns all over the world. If this show ever were to travel that far.

How to arrive? Some take plane rides, while others are happy with a bus ticket. Logan, in the start, on his first show preferred hitchhiking, until that became difficult due to the spread of stranger danger. That didn't matter now, it was too late to worry about any of this would be perceived. In many ways, the truth of the work is already alive and well everywhere electricity was found.

Talking a deep breath, a reality out of awareness started to form around what was about to happen. All the regular signs of show anxiety were there. Particularly early this time, in comparison to the original date but late considering the advancement.

Still, while sitting static, gratitude filled Logan's chest that there was an audience willing to venture into public spaces to see what has happened in the last year of a well undervalued life as an overvalued photographer. Large smiles came when the amount of how lucky he really was developed into a clear picture.

With that feeling possibility, Logan sauntered into action towards all of the preparations needing done. Sauntering, because anything faster might have just killed him. First on the list was to give the publicist a call to inform them that he was alive and planning to go through with the show. Not convinced with cell phones, Logan dialed out from the landline. Ring, ring, ring, "Top Hat publicist, how can I help you?"

"Don, it's me Logan. The pictures will be ready in a few days, I'll mail them to the gallery as soon as the frames and shippers have arrived to prepare the work for transport."

"Logan? You are still with us? Wow, we haven't heard from you in years. Are you still producing work?"

"Yeah Don, do you know I have that show coming up, at that one place down the street from your office? The show, the show about trash? *Trashed*, the exhibition?"

With only the white noise responding for longer than a happy moment, Don came back to the conversation, "Logan, that show was scheduled two years ago, it was cancelled after you never responded to our emails. If I'm being generous, following ample amounts of communication effort, we moved on to someone else. In fact, she has been one of our best success stories. Unlike most, she's a riches to richer story. I tell you, to be born wealthy and then have her talent, a very lucky individual if you ask me."

Again, static was around to rule the conversation. "Don, we both know you were paid off early for agreeing to be my agent."

Laughing, "Look Logan, you're the one that disappeared on some sort of creative spiral. Opportunity knocked once. While you spent the night sleeping off whatever symptoms you caused upon yourself, others have been pushing the envelope. Your chance to show came and went without you."

Logan, completely confused, went to the kitchen fridge to find the calendar to check the dates. The calendar date was correct but on a two year old timeline.

"Don, where did two years go?"

"If I had to guess, you've been hiding out in your home and when you did emerge, you treated all of your friends like trash cans and one by one they left you on the curb. We tried everything man, you just were too far gone to be reached at any given moment."

Buildup of previous momentum dissipated from his bones through the body and eventually affecting his vocals to feet, replacing what voice was left. Not about the mystery show or lost years but a personal dispute about how it could have been scrapped. Being a photographer was who he was. If not that, then all this has been for nothing. Truthfully, all of this has just been some trick of the mind to make his life more grand than reality.

Instead of wrestling with fame, the focus should have been focusing on the slow-burn now representing time. "So, there's no art show? You have anything for me that might fit this timeline? Anything at all?"

Familiar static pitched in the sound of tossing paper. "No Logan, there's not, you have just been gone for too long. Maybe try and sell your work online." Following that, the call was over with Don on the end ending the communication. Sober and alone, the home surrounding the moment went cold. No show ran through his mind until the point it would have scabbed over if emotions could activate in the manner of a cut.

Not only was there not a show but all the trash cans in his personal life stopped talking to him. Settling in after the shots to context, feelings of pity were quick to equate after a while spent staring at the wall thinking about ways to hurt Don. One such way including kidnapping his trash cans but that was the old Logan. The new Logan understood the importance of trash bins and their need for family ties. Besides, dealing with weird Don and whatever he was throwing out was punishment enough.

Finally, he concluded it was time to drink some drugged wine and call galleries himself. Unorthodox but a lot of them have made an unfair killing off photos shown in their establishments. One call, two calls, three, eight calls went by, with unfamiliar interns answering the phone who have never heard of his work and suggested that he apply online or that their space was booked for three years out.

Again, another brick wall that had never been on this road appeared. How hard could it be to get into a reputable gallery? For years it felt like they were everywhere, willing to do whatever it took as long as they got their forty percent. Now, not one space was willing to show his work. Unselected by the community, an ugly terror threatened closing the lid on a career. A headache in a chair belonging to the desk creaked over the artist's body as he leaned back to face what was now a moment of nothing. No shows, no kin to talk to, no obligations. Complete abandonment resulting in the time being, marooned for disillusion.

Weeks into the nothing turned rapidly into two months while showing signs that this forgotten lifestyle might be Logan's new way of executing movement. Sure, at first time was lost but now that has been discovered and since so much of it had been garnished, each moment seemed to matter, that is until it didn't.

It seems like the longer nothing required attention the more focus it took to care about the names of days associated with hours that coexisted with holidays. With the shades down on his column, breakfast ruled dinner while sleep became inactive for it was not essential for a continuum to exist.

Cameras along with their attachments also became unfamiliar to normality. After all, with no shows there was no reason to use them. It was just easier to take the photo within the mind than to figure out where the necessary equipment was stored that provided the power to acquire the moment as a still cry of what happened or not.

Within, an attachment also came for the frustration towards Amber and Hayden, still deciding to remain silent in all of this. There was no way to judge a perimeter of what was really going on. Those two had always been a voice of reason when silence threatened to revoke its right to push him into the field of misdirection. The exact spot where Logan now stood, completely folded towards the unwillingness of his mind to ease up on any little thought that came to, even if the line was only dreaming.

Dangerous towards the overall well-being of just him, like most creative people, the disease to overthink everything was delivered on a deeply personal level that attempted to stay that way unless otherwise delivered through an obsession like taking pictures of trash. Set aside, Logan was happy for the accumulation of sleep now available. Days would go by where only the bed knew if he was alive for in a way most figured he had already expired.

Death was still far away but it's the easiest way to explain someone going from number one to never seen again. Even if Logan was never really missing in action just swamped by a new idea, the required commitment from addicts was hard to understand. Again, who has never been completely overtaken by something in one form or the other? Possibly consider all the ways people suffer from stages of love, family, chemicals and art. Logan gets up to refocus his energy on more positive ideas.

Maybe taking a quick visit out back to see his old friends will help. Opening the back door, Amber and Hayden laid on the ground pulling at weeds that had formed around the fence. Happy to see them animated he greeted them, "Boy, do you two look trashed!" Then, as with any awkward new found idea, he waited for a while after adjusting himself.

"Logan," replied Hayden, "You're in your boxers, holding a pitcher of wine. Maybe you should go inside and eat something?" Both trashcans were sitting upright while looking worried towards the current situation, offering an unfavorable view.

"You idiot, Logan," yelled Amber, "just go inside before there is another incident."

A little shocked by the greeting from the two friends he felt the best action was to give them space, besides, trash day was not for another few rotations of grocery delivery, "Okay, then, you two enjoy gardening."

Logan was all too impressed that Hayden could convince Amber to garden but it's amazing what people can do when asked repeatedly. Even more curious was that Amber did not have a cigarette in her mouth. It was almost like her lips were falling off or her identity was revealed. In any matter, no, they did not want bothered and he did in fact forget to put on pants.

Fully clothed moments later, a thud hits the outside of his door. Upon arrival the door was opened with the slide of a newspaper, laying on top of fellow newspaper corpses now sixty or so piled previously, decomposing from their formal reliability. And older person across the street watering roses yelled over, "Good afternoon Logan, thank you for being clothed this time."

"Just trying to do my part," went Logan. Both nodding nervously while returning quickly to unnecessary tasks in an effort to show the other person they were too busy to actually carry this conversation past a greeting. Retreating rapidly behind the green door to further excommunicate relations, the sound of a lock and deadbolt felt reassuring to him that the outside world had only been exposed for a short moment.

Extra coffee was made then placed into a cup. The display saying something about gratitude and a bagel was made to accompany the moment making seven at night at riot but also breakfast. Unwrapping the newspaper oddly brought attention to the evening. It was clear Logan still might be unhealthily losing time. Shrugging, that's no matter as long as progress was made to better understand what has been going on around him that only a friendly disposal could see.

Removing the paper from the plastic bag that acted as a guardian for the new it stuck to the wooden kitchen table. On the front page there was a giant picture of a confederate soldier statue being removed without the community members being aware. On the right was an ad for a lawyer willing to sue anyone you like for no charge as long as they don't get money from the accused. Last was some sort of ordinance that would prohibit how many signs one placed in their yard or how many flags they can have on display.

In a way it was nice to see that while Logan was out of touch for so many years, the people as a group still were able to truly focus on the big picture. Aside from the page to help sports scores, page three criminal dictations, page four more criminal dictations, a page for fake news, then on another page of for rents around the neighborhood followed by covert advertisements which fed into personal ads. One personal ad really felt unfortunate but that just might be the overall condition of print. The ad read something like this.

In need of a friend willing to share an apartment with the understanding that they are never to be there but other services are tradable. Such being: poetry editing, modeling, writing and painter. Best, Juniper.

Questioning some of those requests, Logan can't help but to think of his old friend that had some sort of ordeal in the theater once. Apparently, a lot was taken from the experience including life, identity and laws that excluded including all types of them, those, they and theirs.

After exploring the possibility of reconnecting with Juniper, Logan instead decided to write them a card once things turned to a place suitable for understanding. Right now would only further pledge of sense of being a victim when in reality they were worth their actions on any day that is forgettable.

Retreating towards the events section, Logan plants hope for an opportunity to show trash. Finding out that most of the events had some sort of political agenda or simply could care less about his kind. In many respects, without a sense of some danger, there was not much for him to partake in. Yeah, a lot of the causes were awesome but at the same intersection that hinged on the downfall of others, in the same way one drowning person uses the other drowning person to elevate himself above the waterline. Survival has always had its accessories even if those succeeding will forever need those facing flight.

Then, there it was. A small twenty five word clip, it started with, *Word Revolt*. Following words spoke of a free gallery that let anyone apply, for free no matter who, what, how or religion. The only consideration was their art and that it be truly helpful. Free to apply, free to show and whatever the sale the artist keeps all.

While living in this town all his life Logan had never heard about this particular gallery. He did suspect social media had done its fair share to block them from the populace but that did not stop the world altogether. With dull scissors the piece was cut out then placed on the fridge by the two-year-old calendar. As soon as his fingertips left the supporting magnet Logan thought to himself, absolutely not again.

Right away the computer was back on, four hours of rebooting then another hour figuring out the internet password belonging to the neighbors, the password for his email, password for the folder containing the images that need to be sent and then five more hours trying to resize the images to fit the email size requirement. All of a sudden it was clear why smartphones felt a sense of superiority. Still, by the end of what felt like days, everything was sent in according to the promises of a very fickle machine.

A day later an email came back from the existing exhibit hall. Expecting another rejection Logan poured a glass of wine or two then opened the letter.

Congratulations Logan,
Your work has been selected for the show, blah blah blah.
All the best, WR

Standing out of being ecstatic, finally! A place to regain transition towards what was once foolishly squandered. Replying with a, "thank you," all that was left was to prepare once again.

With a few more correspondences, Logan was sure to keep the date liquid on his mind. This time he would not forget. Filing away the old calendar while replacing it with a new one from India, this time once again held a stamp. A stone of importance willing to keep what was once unrecognizable in order. Not as great by the sound of it but important to someone keen to be a being lost in a mind full of destructive capabilities.

This show would be a second chance. A rival of the old self that attempts to rescue the new from slipping too far away from what made Logan the person that fell for this craft in the first place. A perfect, small gallery for a rather sharp miniscule returning practitioner to the arts. Ready, everything was set into motion and before too long the date of redemption drew close.

In the meantime, Logan started to explore where his passion originated from. What made him want to capture light in the form of existence? Who was his true love when it came down to shutter speed and shadows? Returning started slow but all these questions came across hard answers followed by soft welcomes back into the community. Logan no longer had to hide but felt exposed towards the truth only crazy people should ignore. Even the neighborhood started to come forth and thank him for not sleeping in their yard anymore.

Strangely, the street on which he lived even started to have less trash cans. At first, there were what felt like thousands, then only a few. Still lingering with particular opinions about relevant topics. After a while or closer to the show, maybe a handful still existed. Some new to the area, others older, hanging on to what they had seen in the past. Overall, there seemed to be a revival.

Amber and Hayden started talking to Logan on a regular basis. Maybe it was the extinction of the tainted wine or newfound direction brought forth by having started again, it did not matter. Today was a gift that Logan O'Lakes planned on remembering. Not only recalling but capturing as well. Taking away the idea that it wasn't important the time or day but the inspiration that made a photo a worthwhile endeavor.

The day of the show, all the wine in the house was drained into a fissure. A quick invite towards Amber and Hayden was offered. Uber called.

Chapter Ten
Exhibit Day

Existing in the back of a stranger's car, it was interesting to no one which direction was more suitable to meet reception requirements. Logan felt the dryness form in his mouth from the lack of troubled waters. Nerves joined in harmony as to ambush the clarity of mind set on delivering a change to create the beginning of another era that focused on people more than what they represented.

Even if their actions correlated with inanimate objects or not. This time, this show was going to feel clean. Miles, three passed, dials, seven past, the driver and Logan only shared practical glances in the rearview mirror.

Unstable with the silence Logan blurted out over the cry of an ambulance, "I'm going to an art show tonight, one of my first in many years. You see, I used to be well known in this environment and now I'm just like all the others, starting fresh in this type of human experience. You would not believe how hard it is to actually put yourself out there for complete strangers, trash cans too. For some people, you'd never guess how hard it is to give them your everything and hope they don't just dump it out one morning, to only fill themselves with other contents until they are full once more."

Sitting back and feeling a sense of relief from talking about this out loud, Logan continued, "Driver, tell me, don't you ever feel like we are all trash cans roaming around, selected as the garbage of society until there's no more room, so we dump out everything from the previous week to make room for the next popular trend?"

Shaking his head Logan went on more eased, "It's like no matter what you do to inspire all of those around you a silly video of a cat will always win, every time unless it's kind of a, 'meme'? Did I say that right? Anyway, art is so digital in a massive way it's become too overwhelmed with content so that attention to detail is completely lost.

Through technology nothing should show human error in its final development. Texture, the last fingerprint of any masterpiece is left flat by electricity. Even my photos might never be able to compete with the program a young person can use through an application. Crazy how when it comes to the creation of fast we were willing to step over the wall of time. It's not long away that it will be writing all of our books if that has not happened already."

Pausing to reflect on the long rant no one asked for, Logan leaned forward to engage the driver further, "So, what do you think?" Nothing. "Hey, so do you have a thought on this? State-of-the-arts, and it's entirety and all the craziness?"

Reaching forward Logan placed his hand on the driver's shoulder, immediately the car shot right over to the median, simultaneously turning off as a driver bolted out from behind the wheel to standing in front of the car. Left in the back seat Logan sat wide-eyed like a deer trying to understand the momentum of a traveling people carrier, stepping out slowly Logan softly reached out with you concerning voice, "Driver, is everything okay? Are you okay? What happened just then?"

With their hand on their watch, the transporter pulled up their hand to their ears and replied, "Police? Yes, my name is Malk, I'm an Uber driver and my passenger is trying to harm me. Our coordinates have been sent."

Logan, standing with questions stumbled and replied, "No, no, no I thought we were just having a conversation? I did not mean any harm towards you, it's okay all I want to do is make it to my art show tonight."

Hands up with his intent the police arrived quickly behind to illuminate the situation in colored lights. "Yeah right mister, you're going to jail you rapist."

"Wait!" yelled Logan, "I am not anything of the sort. All I did was try and engage you in conversation. Didn't your elders ever hold your hand or rub your back to show their love or consideration in the importance of what was being said? All I was trying to do is connect with you on a friendly, human level."

"It's called consent. You paid, you have no right to trespass on my body."

"Trespass? All I was simply trying to do was greet a fellow person with assurance about our time together. The only notion I meant was positive affirmation."

"Whatever you say dude, you are not going to get away with this. Not at least until I take you and your kind down."

"My kind?" spills Logan, "and what is that?"

"People who think it's okay to act however they want towards strangers."

Logan, lowering his hands, "And why are we strangers? Maybe if you took those ear vessels out of your head and actually made the time to understand who I was we both could have gone on to an art show, laugh at jokes and who knows, had a wonderful night of meeting others that have been taught that it's wrong to embrace each other. You know Driver, saying things has always been the perfect way to enlighten people."

Producing a mask out of his pocket, Logan went on, "Amongst other clever distractions, this is really why nothing is alright. We are being torn away from one another in a form of control, an effort to keep us from realizing what is really going on here. You don't have to hate me but are taught to distrust me because of my Irish complexion. Being a male probably doesn't help either but that aside, tonight while your earbuds played criminal satire into your brain.

I told you about my personal fears, heartache. Oh well, you found a conclusion you were fed through people you and I have never met. Meanwhile, the real me is about to spend the night in jail out of popular misconceptions about how people can't communicate through talking about expectations with our relationships. Driver, I mean you no harm. Never will it be okay for those who do, but we will never be able to weed the garden of all the dangerous plants that are altered to have thorns."

The police quickly approached along with life-ending force ready and fluid. Lots of yelling with words that felt forceful followed but would have been silly if set on a higher octave in a song. At this moment, what had happened to the world in the last few years when Logan was hibernating felt important but worth ignoring if this was a new normality called interaction. For the first time, Logan would feel he was not the only one who observed everyone else as trash cans. In fact, on the side of this particular road he saw a dumpster.

"Stop," yelled the driver, "Oh, please stop, this person is okay." Gun still raised enjoying the possibility of sending another Irishman to imprisonment the moment shifted. "No, this creative is correct. Officers, we must stand for justice, not clumping every person into a category just because. This weird individual may have trespassed but on who's antiquated terms? Are they friendly? Could not tell you. Never took the time to listen. And that statement there lies the point. We as a society have stopped taking the time to actually listen to our fellow survivors of what has only begun to be a war brought to us by misdirection. Passenger, what is your name?"

"Logan, my name is Logan and you, driver?"

"Malk, I identify as Malk." Easing up Malk yelled over to the aggressors only doing their job, "It's okay Blue, we just got off on the wrong silence."

After a few tense moments of questions with a temperature cooling pressures from both Malk and Logan, they had to go in order to make it to the show in time, everyone went on their way. Safely, what should have felt aggressive was averted by a simple wisdom of two individuals willing to disagree, learn, then apply their understanding towards the other not seeing them as a stranger riding down the road with them.

From there, Malk and Logan held on to a conversation about art, craft, purpose and predestination. Only this time all of the distractions were off if not removed. Logan also got to sit in the front in effort to make eye contact to help prove the innocence of the moment. The rest of the journey went smoothly ending with the two sharing a small cabernet tucked away in Malk's trunk. Together they had learned the ordeal of being in a pickle that no one should be able to dictate without approval.

Arriving in the small shopping center just in front of the really small gallery, Logan turns to Malk, "Oh, are you sure you don't want to come in and see what you have fought for tonight?"

"No Logan, I don't. If I like it there might be a chance we become friends that would require too much attention from each other's busy day. If it's bad, then regret will inform me that you do actually belong in jail."

Laughing together, Logan understood with a smile. Malk smiled, "Now get out of my car before you try and touch me again. Small grinds ended with a hug as Malk drove to the end neither held towards an expectation.

Walking towards the front door there was a pint sized crowd enjoying what wine and cheese have been left outside for the wondering masses. A happy Southern sounding person welcomes Logan with a big grin that melted into a positive demeanor. After a few moments a bout electricity mixed with overzealous amounts of cheap wine a slender man wearing Chuck's opened the gallery door on his way out to let Logan inside.

Once inside the tiny space felt like a dream that was going to be short but for some reason memorable. If not for the art, then for the museum vibe that's unloaded from the dispersed antiques from a company in New York. Strange and in so many fashions this was nothing like the higher graded galleries Logan was used to.

In fact, the floor had a sticky feel as the tread on it was only painted this morning. Regardless, there were once again, pictures produced, developed, agonized over then delivered hanging on a wall up display. The overhead lights made the moment magical while the dog running under foot felt foreign and maybe even a little third world.

Perfect, absolutely perfect in a way that brought the moment close to feeling oddly familiar. This was not an exhibition as it was more of a gathering of individuals looking to push forward in an addiction all their own. Impulse came to mind later but definitely an act that had a feeling of uncontrollable desire to push. Stuck, wandering familiar voices rang over the word ranch in effort to pull what has begun to back out into the actual moment.

"Logan!" said Amber and Hayden as they simultaneously hugged him. Now understanding the trespassing idea, stepping back from the embrace, Logan gazed in surprise upon two individuals smiling with warm intent. They were no longer trash cans, human to the point of having flesh even though one had a green shirt on while the other a reflective metallic.

Causing enough to raise light concern, "My friends, it's great to finally see you in public looking dashing."

"Same to you Logan, for a few years you worried us. More so when you would toss glass jugs at Hayden like he was some sort of recycle bin." Music carried the awkward truth past the present.

"Yeah, I was just not in the moment you two but thank you for sticking around. And Amber, I see that you quit smoking? That's great."

"Well, Logan, all of those nights of you falling off the normality train made me realize the importance of some self control."

From there, the three friends stood and discussed Logan's return to working for Amber and Hayden, "Look Logan, we know you don't currently have a license but when you do we would like to offer you your old job back driving around the seniors in our care facility. It's not much but at least it will pay for what needs you have today. Maybe, some photo supplies too."

Realizing the trash can hallucinations and famous grandeur of success had been a symptom of losing the handle over a mind bent on escaping reality, Logan humbly accepted the position. With the end of the night rolling through, the last ten minutes chimed with the descent of each onlooker. One by one the first day of a long trail of days has ran its course.

"Excuse me Logan, are you the artist that took these trash photos?" Pointing towards a collection of work dispersed over the room, poorly framed in any material that can be found representing edges of a square.

"Yes, I did take these photos."

The taller person, well-dressed, took a moment to observe the confidence of Logan's response. Leaving much time for other words, the two went on listening to background music of some sort of whimsical band.

"Great," said the taller person, "I'll take them all. I'm going to give a check to the shop owners." They announced before disappearing into the night.

Almost immediately, the room became lighter, the few people remaining became fuzzier while changing shape. Aware of this particular transformation, Logan stood lost then headed for the door landing outside with the hors d'oeuvres, accompanying wine attached to people. Drinking multiple small cups in a row before devouring a bag of chips and then more sinister small cups. That famous warm sensation overtook the rationality most feel important to keep in public gatherings.

Unless you're Logan O'Lakes, famous photographer of trash. One more cup down, a car came screeching to a halt just in front of the gallery. Window down a voice rang, "Logan get in, we have to get out of here!" Smiling, he tossed his cup towards the trash can leaning on the snack table then went headlong into the car just before hearing, "Hey, I'm not a trash can!"

Book by Todd Rykaczewski

2022

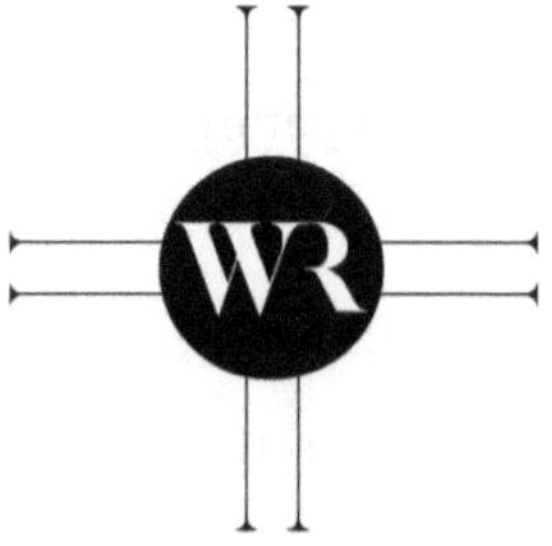

Word Revolt

www.ingramcontent.com/pod-product-compliance
Lightning Source LLC
Chambersburg PA
CBHW061250310726

48971CB00007B/2299